CW00816334

LISTEN

First Published in 2012
Published by Whitebeam Publishing
1 Nightingale Mews
Saffron Walden
Essex
CB10 2BQ

www.whitebeampublishing.co.uk

Designed by Paul Barrett Book Production, Cambridge www.pbbp.co.uk
Whitebeam Publishing logo designed by Joanna Whittle. Copyright © Joanna Whittle
Cover image designed by Dinh Truong Giang. Copyright © Dinh Truong Giang

ISBN 978-0-9571408-1-3

LISTEN

MAGGIE WHITTLE

WHITEBEAM PUBLISHING

*Maggie's dedication with love is to Jo, Stuart,
Don, Rowan, Holly, Mandy and John*

Contents

PART **TWO**
Targeted Metaphorical Stories

Hungry Mouth   73

Come out of denial, face up to the reality of a situation
Free yourself from destructive patterns in your behaviour and from addiction
Participate in life

The Fairy Whose Heart Was Stolen   81

Face fears no matter how scared you are
Overcome childhood trauma and abuse
Find real friendship and love again
Tap into the power of forgiveness

The Ostriches   91

Resist the temptation to please other people at all costs
Accept the generosity of others when you need it badly
Hold onto true power and stand up for yourself
Make healthy relationships with others

The Blue Fairies And The Power Stone   99

Act despite fear; take courage
Speak up for yourself; help others regain their power

The Princess Of Sleep   107

Face life rather than hide away
Let go of false pride, jealousy and resentment
Appreciate others
Live in the present and be happy, rather than wishing your life away

Fire Dance 161
Let go of resentment, grudges and bitterness
Forgive others who are truly sorry
Recover from loss and grief
Develop kindness and compassion
Find love, joy and friendship again

PART
ONE

1
My Experience Of Using Targeted Metaphorical Stories

Targeted Metaphorical Stories offer many great, gentle, enjoyable opportunities for promoting positive changes on all levels. Targeted Metaphorical Stories address a particular topic or problem in a transformative way, representing in narrative form abstract feelings, emotions and behaviours.

For many years, I have created and used Targeted Metaphorical Stories, in both my clinical practice and in self-development training, and I have seen how the stories can enable people to make many quick, remarkable changes.

In groups, participants always smile when I tell them to sit back, get comfortable, close their eyes and relax, while I tell them a story related to the relevant topic. There is no doubt that everyone enjoys a good story, whatever their age or walk of life.

Within a group setting, I find that individuals often want to talk afterwards about the character's predicament in the story, and about how, often without realising it, they too have felt trapped in parallel ways. This realisation, coupled with hearing how the character in the story finds new resources to free himself or herself, motivates and empowers the listeners to take action themselves where needed. *Working with individuals*, either in counselling, hypnotherapy or otherwise, it is always remarkable to see the positive impact that a Metaphorical Story can have on an individual and how quickly, a long-held, unhelpful, rigid view or attitude can begin to, metaphorically, melt away.

2
Role Of Stories In Our Evolution

Stories shape the way we interact with each other and the world. At a basic level, stories entertain us but this same format can be used to educate us, motivate and inspire us, and inform us of current events. They can warn or frighten us, or foster virtues and moral values in us.

Stories and their numerous metaphors and imagery are part of our culture and inheritance and have been recounted by people everywhere throughout history. Stories appeal to people of all ages and walks of life. Without metaphorical stories, communication would be severely restricted, inadequate and very boring.

We obsessively consume stories on a day-to-day basis and some of the narratives we absorb can be less than helpful to our development. For the story has often been used, and continues to be, as a way to foster greed, selfishness and large-scale consumerism. Stories are often used to promote false values, to instil fear and hostility and, generally, to impart untrue or misguided information.

Metaphorical Stories have a profound effect on us because they engage both the left side and right side of our brain simultaneously, targeting both our conscious, rational mind and our unconscious, creative mind.

Engaging both parts of our brain is the most effective way of all to learn and remember.

3
Use Of Targeted Metaphorical Stories In Therapy And Self-Development

Psychologists, life coaches, hypnotherapists, counsellors, health care professionals and educators acknowledge that *positive* Metaphorical Stories are a very effective tool in promoting *positive change* on all levels. Since they offer endless possibilities for imparting knowledge, presenting alternative positive options, and stimulating change at every level, they are extensively used in these settings today. Trainers and development workers in the business field also utilise the powerful tool of Metaphorical Stories to achieve success and advancement.

Targeted Metaphorical Stories can *entertain us, educate us, motivate us,* and *positively shape* how we *view* ourselves, others and the world at large.

Targeted Metaphorical Stories can also *positively shape* how we *relate* to ourselves, others and the world at large.

Targeted Metaphorical Stories play an important role in therapy and self-development because they help individuals *develop more helpful views, attitudes, values and behaviour.*

4
The Power of Targeted Metaphorical Stories

Although Metaphorical Stories appeal to our conscious mind, their use of imaginative metaphors also appeals to our unconscious creative mind. It is within the realm of our unconscious mind that all *our beliefs, views* and *attitudes* are *held.* Our daily lives are influenced by these *beliefs, views* and *attitudes* and they can either work *for us,* enabling us to develop emotionally and spiritually, or they can work *against us,* stifling our emotional and spiritual growth.

> The Metaphorical Stories have the ability to communicate with our unconscious mind *directly.*

They can provide the *information, insight* and *resources* necessary to redress existing *unhelpful views, attitudes* and *behaviour.*

They can offer many *positive* options for dealing with *present* and *future* problems and dilemmas.

5
How Our Childhood Metaphorical Stories Were Formed

As children, we learned how to *feel* about ourselves, about others, and the world around us through the actions and responses of parents and other important adults in our lives. As children, we absorbed and assimilated everything without discernment, the good and the bad, all the information or misinformation we received, all the messages, both positive and negative, that we received.

From the way in which we *perceived* and *interpreted* this information, as children, and the *meaning* we gave to our experiences, we formed beliefs, views, attitudes and behaviour.

These childhood perceptions and interpretations became the blue-print for many of our adult beliefs, views and attitudes.

Our unconscious *beliefs, views* and *attitudes* act as our internal guides.

They tell us how to *view* and *interpret* each situation we encounter.

They tell us how to *feel* about it, how to *react* to it, and how to *deal* with it.

If we, as children, were misinformed or *inadequately* informed about how to *handle* life or *strong emotions*, we may have taken this information on board and made this, too, the *blue-print* to build future patterns on.

Many of the beliefs, views and attitudes we formed in childhood were positive, helpful and beneficial to us as adults. However, many were less than helpful and most of us acquired some unhelpful ones.

Although we may have changed, updated or deleted some of these original beliefs and patterns, many others are still very alive and active today and force us to retain negative ways of viewing ourselves, others and life generally. We may end up with unhelpful reactions and behaviour that let us down and often impact negatively on others, too.

We need to remember that many of our *beliefs, views* and *attitudes* which cause us the most distress, are *not always* based on *truth*. More often than not, they are based on the *misconceptions* and *conclusions* of *childhood* when we had limited understanding.

This is particularly so when it comes to the negative beliefs we formed about ourselves, our worth, our value, our capability and our personal power. Yet our ability to rationalise was not even developed at the time.

Our powerful belief systems, views and attitudes, imprinted in the form of stories, metaphors and imagery in our unconscious mind, provide the blueprint for how we *view ourselves* and *others* and how we *deal* with life on a daily basis, even as adults.

Without our knowledge, they can remain imprinted on our unconscious minds and continue to influence our perceptions and behaviour throughout life. Often, unhelpful views, attitudes and ways of dealing with life events go unchallenged and gain strength unless we deliberately seek to change them. Even as adults, we may perceive them as normal and never even question them. They have been with us so long that we believe in their truth.

Over the years, these imprints become stronger and more deeply rooted, causing us to repeat the same patterns when dealing with situations, over and over again. As a result, certain situations will always make us feel anxious, miserable, sad, angry or guilty.

6
The Impact Of Childhood Stories On Our Emotional Development

The Stories and Metaphors of our childhood, imprinted on our unconscious minds, often leave us with many negative beliefs and misconceptions about ourselves, others and the world generally. Not only will they tell us what *we can* and *can't do* in life, but they will determine the *degree of confidence, self-esteem* and *inner power* we have.

The more unhelpful beliefs and misconceptions we have about ourselves and others, the more open we are to fears and worries, and we may fail to live life to the full or find real happiness. We can be prevented from truly engaging with others, making us feel outsiders in our own lives.

Negative or limiting views and misunderstandings may cause us a high level of anxiety in *certain situations* as adults. We can often feel ill-equipped to deal with powerful and distressing emotions, whilst, in other aspects of our lives, we may be very capable, competent and successful.

Our inability to cope with conflict, anger, hurt, rejection, jealousy, grief and other strong emotions can hinder us in our daily lives when certain situations arise. If we still adhere to unhelpful childhood patterns, we open ourselves up to a lot of stress and unhappiness. We may even develop new fear ridden and untruthful views about ourselves and others.

Unhelpful unconscious imprints can leave us with loss of confidence and a poor self-image as well as an ever-growing set of beliefs and behaviour that tallies with our old ingrained patterns. Our unhelpful ways of dealing with life events will mirror this, and we shall be continually impeded by our unconscious beliefs. Very few of us escape having some misguided views and patterns that hold us back in certain aspects of our lives.

Targeted Metaphorical Stories are a quick, yet profound and enjoyable, way to break free from unhelpful, often unconscious, views and behaviour.

They are a quick way to develop many healthy options, which will give us a greater sense of freedom and self-empowerment.

7
What These Fifteen Targeted Metaphorical Stories Offer

These stories *target* many of our common human dilemmas, upsetting experiences, distressing emotions and unhelpful behaviour as outlined in the Contents.

If the reader or listener of the story is facing a similar dilemma as that of the character in the story, they will feel less isolated and alone with their own problem as all humans benefit from identification and solidarity with others. They will feel empathy with the character who is suffering the same kind of distress as themselves. This will enable the individual to make more sense of their own feelings and behaviour without feeling inferior and isolated.

The beneficiary of these stories will be able to travel through the experience with the various characters, sharing their defeats, distressing feelings and the obstacles that hold them back. They will be able to see how the characters have become trapped in an unhappy place. Thus, once the characters find ingenious and creative ways of dealing with their distressing emotions or problems and free themselves from the situations, the individual, too, will be able to see ways of transforming their own situation. They will be able to see a way out of their own unhelpful views and patterns to find freedom themselves, and will be able to experience the same sense of relief and empowerment that these new ways of coping bring.

These new ways of viewing and dealing with problems and situations, which hitherto seemed hopeless, will offer the individual many new possibilities and creative resources for building future helpful thought patterns and behaviour.

As well as being enjoyable, Targeted Metaphorical Stories are one of the most powerful and gentle tools used today in the field of psychology, education and self-advancement for promoting change and development.

Weaved throughout the light-hearted stories are wise insights, brief, necessary information, life skills and resources that will promote positive changes on many different levels.

8
About Each Particular Story

Each Metaphorical Story has its own *specific topics and themes,* as outlined in the chapter contents. All have multi-layered metaphors and operate on many different levels. Each story will help individuals *recognise* clearly, and then, break out of specific unhelpful views, attitudes and behaviour.

● Each story offers new perspectives and insights into *specific* situations, dilemmas and behaviour and provides the recipient with more *skills and resources* to deal with them in the best possible way.

● They help individuals identify and understand their own emotions better. This will enable them deal better with intense or frightening feelings such as fear, rage, anger, shame, strong guilt or grief.

• Each story provides individuals with the ability to *update or change* unhelpful, often unconscious, views, attitudes and behaviour patterns.

All the stories promote self-reflection and self-awareness, empathy, personal responsibility, emotional resourcefulness and creative thinking.

All build confidence, self-esteem, positive attitudes and behaviour.

Individuals will gain empowering life skills and insights and improve relationships with themselves and others.

9
How These Stories Can Be Used To Good Effect

These stories can be of great benefit when used either by individuals or in group settings.

They can benefit *any individuals* interested in their own self-development either to increase their life skills and emotional resources or find more helpful ways to *deal* with a specific problem or negative experience.

They can be a great resource for older children and young adults to help them understand their emotions and gain more skills and resources to deal better with specific upsetting experiences such as being bullied or rejected.

Parents can not only benefit themselves but use this great resource to help their child develop more emotional strengths and life skills.

They have been found to be extremely useful for anyone working in the field of mental and emotional health, such as health care workers, therapists, counsellors and nurses. They are also a useful resource for teachers, educators, and youth workers addressing any of the topics covered.

These stories have proved their worth in many different group settings when addressing topics such as overcoming anxiety and fears, being assertive, dealing with bullying and conflict, overcoming bitterness and resentment, developing better relationships, getting over grief, loss or rejection, developing courage, fairness and compassion, co-operation with others and overcoming addiction.

They can be read by anyone just for the enjoyment of reading a good story and the reader will always get new insights.

How To Select A Suitable Metaphorical Story

Each story is preceded by a brief summary of some of the topics it addresses and its possible developmental uses.

Choose a relevant story from the list of chapters under Contents.

10
Suggestions Regarding Reading The Stories

- Just as reading a whole collection of stories in one go would overload the senses, reading this book of Targeted Metaphorical Stories from cover to cover would reduce their effectiveness.

- Once you have chosen a story to read, find a nice, comfortable place for yourself and take a few relaxing breaths and read your story slowly.

- After reading a story, it would be very beneficial to spend time focusing on its message and how to apply that message to your life.

- The story can be re-read many times, offering different insights and options each time.

PART
TWO

Fiachra's Treasures

The Story Of Fiachra's Treasures Shows Us That:

- We can be robbed of our confidence, hopes and dreams by the callous treatment at the hands of others.

- This can leave us feeling fearful, grieved, ashamed and powerless.

- The feelings of powerlessness and shame can make us hide our real feelings from others.

This Story Helps Us To:

Face our worst fears

Recover from past or present hurt, loss, trauma, shame and humiliation

Reclaim our own true power

Become stronger as a result of our bad experiences

Fiachra's Treasures

It was a cool spring morning when Fiachra decided to go on a long journey. He was a much-loved young man with many dreams and hopes. He had already travelled far and wide across the Land of the Seven Seas, collecting many *Treasures*. These *Treasures* would allow him to have the most eventful, wonderful journey of his life. As he sat on a big round boulder, watching the sun rise over the mountains, he listed his *Treasures* to himself:

There was his *Treasure of courage.*

There was his *Treasure of faith and self-belief.*

There was his *Treasure of hope.*

There was his *Treasure of joy and laughter.*

There was his *Treasure of self-love and kindness.*

There was his *Treasure of endurance and freedom of spirit.*

He smiled to himself – he did indeed have many *Treasures* and this would be a wonderful journey. He set off to the east, running, his heart was so full of eagerness to see the world.

Fiachra travelled across mountains, swam across deep rivers, slept in the hot sun. He spent many happy days amongst the red seals on the Barzouka Coast, where the sixth sun rises golden above the golden sea. He spent three days trying to catch moon beetles in Surin. In Tarbok, he met a Jentie priest whose hair was so long, it was half the height of his body when it was rolled on top of his head. Fiachra saw many wonderful things and this was only the beginning; he had so much still to see. His heart filled with joy and his *Treasures* grew brighter when he thought about what had passed and what was yet to come.

One night, as Fiachra slept under a huge plane tree, some thieves fell upon him. They took his food, they took his silver and they took his special golden ring given to him by his loving mother. But, worst of all, these vicious thieves put an *evil spell* on his *Treasure of courage*. Their spell prevented him from seeing, let alone using, his *Treasure of courage*. Without this *Treasure*, he had felt afraid, very afraid indeed – more afraid than he ever had felt in his life.

"All is not lost," Fiachra thought to himself once the thieves had cleared off, "at least I still have my other *Treasures*." But Fiachra very quickly discovered that, although the spell was only on his *courage Treasure*, the loss of his *courage Treasure* denied him *access to* any of his other *Treasures*.

His heart felt crushed and torn in his chest when he realised he had lost his Treasure of *faith and self-belief* because now he *no longer believed* that it was possible to get his *Treasure of courage* back.

He lost his *Treasure of hope* because he *lost hope* of ever finding a way to get his Treasure of *courage* back.

The loss of his *courage Treasure* made him *sad and empty* and so he had no way of getting to his *joy and laughter Treasure*.

His *love and kindness Treasure* was out of his reach, too, because he no longer *felt love* for himself or others; instead, he felt guilty, angry and *deeply ashamed.*

His *Treasure of freedom* was gone because his heart now *felt trapped*, like a small bird caught in barbed wire.

In short, all his *Treasures* seemed to be connected to his *courage Treasure* and now he could not reach any of them. He fell to his knees in the sand and wept bitterly for the loss of his *Treasures*. He felt hopeless, ashamed, lost, lonely and very afraid – more afraid than he had ever been before.

"Oh, if only I could break the spell!" he cried aloud over and over again into the silent night. He was in the blackest despair without even a flicker of hope in his heart.

"I know a way to get your *Treasures* back," whispered a tiny voice beside his right ear.

Fiachra's head jolted up and he looked all around, but saw nothing in the moonlight.

"But you might not like it," said the voice again, this time in his left ear.

"Where are you? Who are you?" he whispered.

In reply, a tiny little fairy fluttered in front of his eyes.

"I am Leyla, I know how to get your *Treasures* back. I saw what those wicked thieves did to you."

"Oh Leyla, if you can help me in any way, please tell me. I am so lost, alone and broken without my

Treasures, I would do anything to get them back, *anything*."

"Listen carefully," said the fairy, Leyla, "the spell those evil people put on you was called the *secret spell*. It's one of the worst spells ever but "*there is a way* to break it." The fairy produced a scroll from the sleeve of her golden dress. On the scroll was written "You have to reveal *the secret* and only then can the spell be broken. Then, and only then, will you be able to reclaim your trapped *Treasures*." Without another word, the fairy fluttered her silver wings and disappeared into the night.

"But, Leyla, Wait!" Fiachra shouted. But it was too late; she was already gone.

Fiachra sat on the ground with his head in his hands and wept quietly. It all seemed too much. It was easy for her to say "Tell the secret" but that's just the thing he couldn't do. He was so afraid. If he told *the secret*, everyone would say he was unworthy, they would say he was a coward. His shame was already suffocating him without adding to it. They would ask him how he could let anyone do such a thing. They would know he had no *Treasures* any more. He would be exposed with nowhere to hide. Surely everyone has to have somewhere to hide, he told himself. Surely he would just disintegrate with shame and humiliation if people knew the *evil secret*. He would never be able to tell anyone what had happened to him. Surely he was justified in that? How would anyone ever look him in the eye again if they knew? No, he decided, it was best to keep quiet and pretend he still had his *Treasures.*

Fiachra broke out into a cold sweat and his whole body began to tremble and shake uncontrollably. He felt sick. He wanted to run away from himself but the words of the fairy went round and round like a song in his head. "To break the *evil spell,* you have to reveal *the secret* and only then will you get your *Treasures* back." Now other thoughts grew and crowded in his head. What if the fairy was wrong? What if she was trying to humiliate and destroy him completely? Wasn't it just safer to hold on to the *secret*? He knew that, once the *secret* was out, he could never hide again.

In the morning, weak and exhausted, he set off to climb the mountain to see the Master. He didn't know exactly when in the night he made the decision to go up the mountain. He felt that, at some time in the darkness of the still night, the decision was made and he held it.

Going up the mountain was torturous for Fiachra. Every step up the mountain filled him with greater fear. His mental anguish affected him physically and he had to force himself up the mountain. Someone had told him the Master was wise but he had no proof of that. It could be another trick to deceive him.

When he finally reached the top, he saw the Master standing still and gazing down the mountain. The Master looked fierce and grotesque. Big warts hung about his face and his voice was harsh and accusing.

"What do you want, young man?" the Master barked. "Speak up, speak up, I can't hear you."

"I came," Fiachra replied in a terrified voice, "to reveal a secret."

"What secret?" demanded the Master, scowling at Fiachra.

Fiachra felt sheer terror and the words stuck in his throat. His face burned hot with shame and guilt.

"I was attacked," Fiachra finally managed to get out, his head hanging down in shame, "they stole from me and cast a spell on my *Treasure of courage*. Now I can't even reach any of my other *Treasures*."

"Go on," roared the Master, "attacked by how many?"

"Four men," replied Fiachra, crying.

Fiachra didn't care anymore and he went on sobbing.

"What did you do to defend yourself?" demanded the Master.

"Nothing," replied Fiachra, "I was so afraid, I couldn't move, I did nothing to defend myself, nothing at all."

"Nothing at all?" asked the Master gruffly.

"Nothing."

Fiachra stopped trembling, he raised his head and a strange peace came over him. He looked up at the Master and saw that his face had changed and was beautiful, gentle and wise. The warts on his face began to change, too, and disappear – butterflies floated from his mouth and took to the air.

The Master began to cry and reached out his hand to Fiachra. "You are a brave man, Fiachra, a very courageous man indeed," the Master said. "You have even greater *Treasures* now. How could you have defended yourself against such evil men? You have shown great bravery in coming here and breaking the *secret spell* despite feeling such great terror and shame. The *secret spell* is broken now; you truly have reclaimed your *Treasure of courage*. All your other Treasures will now fly back to you. You without doubt are a courageous man. Many people live in fear and shame as a result of carrying such a *secret spell* and die carrying the *secret spell* to the grave. You are a real hero."

Again the Master cried. Then he wiped his eyes and slowly rose up onto the balls of his feet. He walked towards his old wooden hut, turning back to look at Fiachra.

"Take time to enjoy your recovered *Treasures* while I knock us up some tasty food. You need a hearty meal, you have come very far."

Fiachra sat on the mountain top and looked down at the valleys and peaks below. A mist was hanging above the treetops which gave the impression of a soft, swirling sea surrounding the mountain. As he gazed into the soft mist, he saw his *Treasures* one by one taking their rightful place in his heart again. His heart sang of them from the mountain top. The Master heard the singing and began to laugh and dance around the mountain, clicking his heels and clapping his hands.

As the bright pink lo-li-ti flowers on the mountain top blushed a glowing crimson in the soft fading mist, Fiachra now knew the colour of *courage.* It was with a happy heart and a light step that Fiacra continued on his eventful journey.

Commander

The Story Of Commander Shows Us That:

- We can have false pride and believe we are superior to others.

- We can be selfish and think only of our needs.

- This can prevent us from making genuine relationships with others.

- We can put others on a pedestal, over-depend on them and fail to develop our abilities.

This Story Helps Us To:

Stand up for ourselves and reclaim our inner strength

Make healthy relationships with others and work co-operatively together with them

Develop our own resources and talents

Develop honour and sound values

Develop compassion for our own and others' weakness

Commander

Alarge flock of Peacocks lived in the vast gardens of the King's palace. This famous King was called *The Mighty One,* so great was his power in the land. His royal subjects bowed and trembled before him. His gardens reflected his great wealth and power. He had a whole team of gardeners to keep the orchards brimming with fruit, which were of the finest species. Accordingly, his Peacocks that roamed freely around these great gardens were the finest specimens in the land.

The Peacocks were proud of their royal gardens and strutted about, displaying their beautiful feathers, to the delight of the King and his courtiers. The fame of the Peacocks spread throughout the land and many visiting rulers came to see their wonderful displays. One proud Peacock stood taller than all the rest. The King named this prize Peacock "Commander" and the King had only to call his name and Commander would strut up and down proudly before him.

Commander strutted around with his wonderful, colourful feathers on display all the time. The lady Peacocks admired him and courted his favour. He would proudly jump up on their backs and implant his royal seed in them. "Another fertilised egg!" he would announce proudly to the envious male Peacocks, who looked on helplessly. The King and his royal courtiers would watch these displays with much admiration for this prize Peacock. The King would declare:

"Ah, I shall have such a strong breed of Peacocks in the future. People will come from far and wide, begging me to sell some to them and offering only the highest prices."

Over time, the hen Peacocks became disgruntled and irritated with Commander, who lorded it over them. Once, they had found his attentions exciting; now they found they were angry and irritated with him. However, they were too embarrassed to reveal how they felt to each other or do anything about it. The male Peacocks were jealous and angry with Commander, too. He deprived them of fathering baby Peacocks and they felt robbed of this, their right. No matter how they strutted, they were no match for Commander and never attracted the attention of the hens.

However, all this strutting and fathering was a lot of hard work for one Peacock. Commander gradually began to grow thinner and thinner. He was overdoing it. He was afraid to rest or eat in case some other Peacock stole his thunder. So it happened that, on one bright sunny day, a great catastrophe struck Commander. For no obvious reason he just keeled over, breaking his wing as a result. There he lay on the ground in the bright sunlight, head pressed into the earth, beads of sweat glistening on his bright feathers, looking bewildered and frightened. His wing was bent back and broken and a sharp piece of broken bone stuck out at an odd angle. He began to whimper and cry out for help.

The other Peacocks gathered around and were excited and delighted at his downfall. They began a vicious attack on him, pecking cruelly at his flesh and plucking out some of his long, beautiful, iridescent blue and green feathers. The female Peacocks joined in the attack, cackling with a vengeance. Commander lay dying and bleeding beneath their onslaught. The King and his royal courtiers strolled past and when the King spotted the attack of the other Peacocks on Commander, he stopped to watch.

"What a performance!" he laughed. "Most spectacular, most spectacular, indeed. Oh well, I shall have to select the next best *strutter* as my prize Peacock."

Commander's heart was crushed and broken by the King's words.

A small Peacock with brilliant plumage, called Bran, jumped on top of Commander with his wings outstretched to protect him from the attacking Peacocks.

"Leave him alone!" shouted this small Peacock. "He is my father and he must be left to die with dignity."

The attacking Peacocks dispersed one by one. Bran dragged his dying father to safety and laid him under a great yew tree for shade and protection. Bran carried some water from the nearby fountain, bathed Commander's bleeding head, gave him some water to drink and collected some choice oat and barley seeds for him. He rarely left his father's side for seven days and seven nights. On the seventh night, Commander stood up for the first time and stretched out his great wings. The wing that was broken stood out at an odd angle and the protruding bone resembled a sharp spear. But, other than that, he had made a full recovery.

As father and son were standing under the yew tree in the silver moonlight, they spotted a cunning fox creeping up on them. The foxes were hungry because a lack of rain had led to scarcity in the land. Without warning, Commander flew at the fox, prancing in front of him, aiming his broken wing with the protruding bone at his face. Like a boxer, he jabbed the razor-sharp broken bone into the fox's nose. The fox yelped in pain and took off at great speed. Commander stretched out his wings and said:

"Look, my dear son, I am now a soldier, a warrior soldier, and it is all thanks to you. Without your bravery and kind heart, I would be dead. You, too, are a real soldier."

Bran's heart swelled with pride.

Commander and Bran went back to live among the Peacocks. Each night, the hungry foxes came to steal a Peacock and each night, Commander attacked and sent the foxes away yelping. As each night drew near, the other Peacocks silently sought out close proximity to Commander for protection from the hungry foxes.

It was about this time that all the Peacocks overheard the King talking about the scarcity coming to his land. The King said he would give a great feast in the near future and invite all the Kings and Rulers from other Kingdoms around. He needed to win favour with them. The King said he would have all the Peacocks killed and served up to his guests to impress them. He knew that his Peacocks were the envy of others.

The Peacocks were dismayed and frightened by this news. They huddled close to Commander and his son Bran. Commander called them all to a secret meeting in the moonlight.

"We must escape or we shall be slaughtered," Commander told them. "We have grown lazy, we have grown flabby, our muscles are weak, we are defenceless and we have almost forgotten how to fly. I shall teach you all how to fly and fight again. My brave son Bran here will teach us how to be brave. We have become cowardly and soft and have allowed ourselves to be tricked. We have to learn these things by night when we shall not be noticed by the palace guards."

He paused to look at the Peacock faces before him; their eyes were wide with fear in the moonlight.

"All those who want to be soldiers, stand to my right!" he called out with a very strong voice.

All the Peacocks ran to Commander's right.

"All who do not want to be brave, leave my right side and go to the left."

Not one single Peacock went to the left.

"Good," said Commander, "we can learn to be both soldiers and brave."

Night after night, the Peacocks could be seen drilling and marching to Commander's orders. He himself drilled and marched with the other Peacocks. Bran talked of bravery and honour to the Peacocks. He taught them about standing up for themselves and for each other. He taught them how to speak up for the truth always. He taught them how to defend themselves and encourage the helpless and weak. Commander taught the Peacocks how to pull out their long tail feathers and use them as swords. Their flying practice and lessons paid off. Soon the Peacocks were flying for longer and longer periods at night. They were also flying higher and higher with ease and grace.

The King arranged the date for his great feast. The Peacocks on *look-out* listened to every word the King and courtiers spoke. The Peacocks learned of the day they were going to be slaughtered. That very day, they gathered together, waiting for the King to walk into the garden. They had not long to wait before they saw the King and his courtiers making their way to the spot where they stood waiting.

"This is the last day of your freedom," the King announced to the Peacocks as he wagged a Royal finger at them. "Tomorrow, you will be my dinner and the dinner of all the high and mighty ones for miles around. What a feast you will make! I can see you now on the silver platters, nicely roasted with your drum-sticks in the air. I guess you have served your purpose, anyhow."

The King looked pleased with himself and his courtiers smiled in appreciation of his speech.

The Peacocks remained silent and attentive with their eyes fixed on Commander. At a signal from Commander, the Peacocks took to the air in majestic flight, leaving the King open-mouthed and furious.

The Peacocks never looked back but flew on to a faraway forest of sunlit plenty. Here, they lived happily and peacefully with each other and were able to defend themselves and their young with great honour and pride. Commander and his son Bran are revered among the Peacocks to this day.

A Gift From The Moon

The Story Of A Gift From The Moon Shows Us That:

- Expecting or allowing others to take responsibility for us impairs our development.

- We may blame everyone else rather than accepting our own mistakes and learning from them.

- Taking responsibility for ourselves enables us to develop on all levels.

This Story Helps Us To:

Appreciate the gifts that we have been given, and look after them

Learn whatever lessons we need to from our mistakes

Face up to personal responsibility

Develop our talents, abilities and resources

A Gift From The Moon

Far across the sea, many years ago, there could be seen rising out of the waves a beautiful island, gleaming gold and white in the sun. It was said that, at one time, the people of this island were able to stretch out their arms and fly up to the moon. However, things had changed since the beginnings of the island and its people could no longer fly to the moon. No one ever spoke of what had caused such a tragic loss of flight but something had happened, which had deprived them of this ability. Each night, the earth-bound islanders would dream of flying to the moon again. But, alas, they were only dreams.

Still, the people who lived on this island were happy and peace-loving. They lived communally and each person, young and old, male and female was respected. Daily, the islanders played games in the sea with giant sea mammals that sprayed jets of water high into the air. They rode big white waves to shore like chariot-racers. They sang dirges and sweet melodies together around night fires. Young and old danced to the beat of drums.

Throughout the hot day, they gathered food together and in the evening, all of the islanders sat beneath the red sinking sun, telling stories and sharing their food. They filled themselves with silver fish caught from the plentiful seas by the young men and ripe figs plucked from the trees by the children and their grandparents.

The children liked the figs and juice ran down their chins as they ran between the legs of the elders, trying to catch fireflies. The women caught shellfish and big yellow beach crabs, which they would roast on the fire.

The islanders' lives fell short of paradise in just one respect: as the sun sank below the sea and the moon and stars appeared in the clear night sky, the island would turn very cold indeed. Whilst food and resources were plentiful on the island, the people had no clothes to keep themselves warm. People huddled together at night to keep warm but no matter how close together they slept, it was never enough to protect them from the biting, freezing night winds. They built large fires but there was only so much wood they could take without destroying the fruit bearing trees. Every night, the fires would go out and the people would awake shivering with cold. Like penguins, they would take it in turns to sleep on the outside of the circle, keeping the others warm. They survived each night like this and sometimes they thought the nights would never ever end and their hearts would freeze inside their chests and stop beating. When the sun rose each morning, they quickly forgot the cold night's torture. They would warm up quickly and start celebrating and singing until once again joy filled their hearts.

One night, when the moon was full and more yellow than ever before and the stars shone more brightly than ever before, the islanders grew colder than they had ever been. They huddled closer for comfort and warmth. The piercing, biting cold winds went right through their bodies and into their bones making them ache and tremble violently. Children cried and moaned piteously. Salty tears flowed silently from the eyes of adults who could do nothing to warm themselves, each other or their children.

It was that very same night that the Moon Goddess appeared. She came gliding through the heavens right from the heart of the moon. Her long hair sparkled silver in the moonlight. She was tall and elegant, graceful-looking and powerful. She had a beautiful smile on her face and piercing, bright, shiny eyes. Around her shoulders, covering her whole body, hung the most magnificent shimmering blue and silver cloak that seemed to sparkle and dance with a life of its own.

The people had never seen the Moon Goddess before. Her face lit up with great joy and she reached out her hands towards the silent people. The children abruptly ceased their moaning and their bodies became still as though transfixed in the presence of the Moon Goddess. Adults, too, became still and stared silently, wide-eyed and awed. No one spoke a word. The people felt as if the heat of warm sunshine were touching their bodies lovingly.

The chill in their bones gave way to warm loving sensations.

Without any prompting or organising, the people formed a circle around the Goddess. The Moon Goddess walked around the circle, laying her hands on the shoulders of each individual. As she did so, a beautiful cloak grew around their body. Each cloak shimmered and sparkled and was as beautiful as the Goddess' own. The fabric felt like skin, it was so warm, so comforting, and it seemed to take on the shape of, and move with, the body of its wearer.

She told the people that the cloak was sensitive to body temperature. If they were too cold, it would keep them warm and if they were too warm, it would keep them cool. She told the people that the cloak was a gift from the moon and as long as they took care of it, it would last forever. The people were extremely happy and gave thanks for their wonderful gift. The Moon Goddess bade them farewell and flew back to the bright moon.

The days and the nights passed and the people were ecstatically happy. At night, the cloaks kept them as warm as rabbits in their burrows and, during the day, the cloaks kept their skin cool and stopped the sun from burning them. They wanted for nothing now and their lives carried on in peace and contentment. The people took care of their precious cloaks, smoothed them out regularly and washed off any dirt. The cloaks always held their shape and never seemed to get holes in them.

However, as time went by, one young man and a woman started to neglect their cloaks. Timel and Rano were too busy splashing in the sea, eating figs and letting their beautiful bodies become golden in the sun.

"Why should we bother?" Timel said to Rano. "The Moon Goddess said our cloaks would last forever anyway."

Rano agreed and lay back in the sun. They trampled on their cloaks, ate while sitting on their cloaks, rubbed the dirt off their faces with their cloaks and generally neglected them. Gradually, contrary to Timel's assertion, their cloaks started to go hard, split, rip and finally disintegrate. It would seem that their cloaks would not last forever without care, after all.

Timel and Rano were dismayed at seeing their cloaks disintegrate. They cried bitter tears when they were together. When they were with the other islanders, they hid their tears. Secretly, they felt angry and ashamed of neglecting their cloaks. At times, they tried to blame other people for not giving them sufficient warning that this could happen. They even shouted up at the Moon Goddess in the sky for not having been more specific in her warning. They begged and pleaded with other people to give them a cloak at night or to let them share one. The people were angry with them for not respecting the Moon Goddess's wishes but they still shared their cloaks with them on particularly cold nights.

One morning, when the people woke from sleep, they saw beautiful little carefully-cut pieces of cloak laid out beside them. The people were astonished and amazed as to where these pieces could have come from. They consulted among themselves as to what to do with the little pieces of cloak. They were happy with this new gift and, after the pieces had appeared three mornings in a row, they realised that new cloaks could be made for Timel and Rano.

It was agreed that the women who could sew well would gather these beautiful pieces and sew them bit by bit so that, eventually, they would end up with two new cloaks.

All day long, several women sewed little pieces of cloak together with their neatest stitches. They went to sleep that night, feeling satisfied, leaving the sewn pieces of cloak beside them so that they could continue sewing the next day. When they woke up, to their dismay, the sewn cloak pieces had grown hard and disintegrated as if they had never been sewn. The people were confused and fearful because the pieces had felt beautiful the day before just like their own cloaks.

The people called a meeting about the disintegrating pieces of cloak. The circle was quiet that night and everyone talked amongst themselves in hushed voices, trying to decide what it meant and what they should do. No one seemed to come up with a solution.

All of a sudden, two little children came bounding into the centre of the circle, startling the elders. The elders were surprised, as the rest of the children were down on the beach, chasing the night crabs and keeping out of the way of the adults, who seemed strange to them that night. The elders recognised the two children as Hum and Dance, twin brother and sister, just seven years old. The boy twin got the name *Hum* because he went around humming all the time. His hum was the most beautiful sound on earth and his sister *Dance* could spin and twirl in the air to this hum as no other ever could. She seemed as light as a feather and as free as any bird.

It was the custom of the people that, if somebody had something important to say, he or she would stand in the centre of the circle. The people were very surprised that the brother and sister had something important to add, as they hadn't even been in on the meeting. Hum stepped forward and announced in a clear voice:

"Timel and Rano who disrespected their cloaks need to collect the cloak pieces *themselves* and sew the cloaks *themselves*, otherwise, the cloak pieces will perish again and die." Dance nodded her head vigorously in agreement.

"But we can't sew," whined Timel and Rano.

"Some of the women can teach you – the grandmothers can teach you – *only you* can sew the cloaks because *only you* abused and neglected your cloaks," announced the child, Dance. Both twins then turned on their heels and ran off to join the other children. The people could hear Hum's favourite tune wafting up from the beach. The people looked at each other, a little surprised, but decided that, since no one else could come up with any better solutions, they would take the children's advice.

So the people went to sleep that night and again, when they woke up, they found new little pieces of cloak nearby. In silence, Timel and Rano collected all the little pieces of cloak and the grandmothers started teaching them how to sew the pieces together. With a lot of struggling, they each managed to sew a part of a cloak. The next morning, all the pieces they had stitched had moulded themselves perfectly to form the beginning of two cloaks. Timel, Rano and the islanders were delighted and amazed.

Each night, the Moon Goddess left her gift of the pieces of cloak and, each day, Timel and Rano gathered up the little pieces and continued to sew until two complete cloaks were made.

When the last piece was sewn, the cloaks moulded together and were as perfect as all the other cloaks. The people sat together and wondered what lesson might be drawn from this strange experience. Timel and Rano certainly knew that they would always treat their brand-new cloaks with the greatest care.

As the elders watched them wrapping their cloaks around themselves, their eyes shining with joy, they called Hum and Dance to them. "How did you know what to do?" they asked them. Both children pointed a finger towards their heart and Dance whispered with a smile, "It's written in there, right in the middle of the heart; you all just forgot to look." The twins giggled and twirled as they made their way towards a pair of nesting sunbirds in the high rocks.

It was only one year and a day later, to be exact, that the people of the Island of Dreams began to fly again. At first, their efforts were slow and clumsy and, like albatrosses, they needed a good run to take off. During these times, they were covered in cuts and bruises from colliding into each other or crash-landing. At times, they cried and at times, they rolled about, laughing and clapping each other on the back. With dedicated practice, they perfected their flying skills and grew graceful in flight.

Now they can be seen at night, gliding around the starry skies with their shimmering, sparkling cloaks floating around their bodies and their joy and laughter echoing above the Island.

The Broken Nest

The Story Of The Broken Nest Shows Us That:

- Sometimes we may have to face painful emotions in order to resolve our relationship with others.

- Avoiding open, honest communicating in relationships is detrimental.

- Although we may be grief-stricken when a relationship ends, in time, many new happy possibilities open up to us.

This Story Helps Us To:

Find the courage to be open and honest in our relationships.

Accept help when we need it.

Recover from loss, grief and rejection when a relationship ends

Find joy and happiness again.

The Broken Nest

B lue Bird found a mate whose name was Silver Flyer. She wanted to nest, lay eggs and bring up her young. Her mate agreed that it was a good idea and they built together a beautiful cosy nest in an old barn. It was a great pleasure for the birds to build a nest together and they spent many happy hours, searching out feathers, leaves, moss, twigs and mud to make their nest secure, cosy and warm.

When Silver Flyer saw the swallows playing merrily in the sky without a care, he became very restless and discontented inside. At first, he ignored this uncomfortable feeling but it was always lurking there somewhere in his mind. Soon, he began to fear the beautiful feathered nest and everything that it stood for. He couldn't eat, he couldn't sleep. Silver Flyer desperately wanted to tell Blue Bird how he felt but the very thought of doing this terrified him even more, so he kept silent. The happier that his bride seemed to become, the more distressed Silver Flyer became. One day, he was so distressed about his unhappy relationship that he became ill and was unable to fly.

"Whatever is the matter? I am so worried about you," wept Blue Bird.

Silver Flyer shrieked between great sobs, "I want to be free and fly to new places, see new things, make long journeys to far-away countries, and rest in new branches out under the stars! I don't want a family. I don't want to wait for eggs to hatch and look after young. I only want to fly and be free."

Poor broken-hearted Blue Bird pleaded, cried, begged and reasoned with her mate. It was all to no avail. Silver Flyer panicked, his heart racing and pounding in his chest, and as he launched himself into frantic flight from the barn, he accidentally knocked Blue Bird onto the barn floor, breaking her wing. He soared into the clear blue sky, his heart fluttering in sorrow and fear.

Blue Bird lay still on the empty barn floor, feeling helpless, weak, shocked and ready to die. Two big tears coursed down her beak and fell onto her beautiful blue iridescent feathers. Her tiny heart fluttered madly in her chest, as if it were trying to escape such deep sorrow.

A little mouse that lived in a small hole in the barn saw her fall and crept up to her. "Don't die, don't die," she said, "I know how to help you. I shall bring you food – good grain from the barn next door. I shall help you to a secure place in the barn where no harm will come to you. I shall be your friend for as long as you need a friend and I shall help you as long as you need my help."

With that, the little mouse scurried away, only to return a few minutes later with some grain. Blue Bird wept as if her heart would break, right there where she still lay. With a gentle coaxing from Mouse, Blue Bird ate the grain and allowed the mouse to drag her to a more secure place in the barn. Mouse visited Blue Bird every day, many times a day. She brought her family to visit, hoping that Blue Bird would be comforted by her little ones, but Blue Bird would not be comforted and cried most of the time. She wailed to the mouse:

"I am all alone, I have no nest now, I have no eggs, no family and no love of my own. It is too much to bear – too much to bear. The barn door is closed now and I am trapped forever." She tucked her head beneath her good wing and wept loudly.

"No, no," said Mouse, "you are getting better, your wing is improving. When you are completely well, my little ones and I shall make a hole for you under the door so that you can get out."

The mice worked night and day, gnawing away at the wooden door, making the hole bigger in readiness for Blue Bird's flight. Blue Bird watched quietly, trying to stretch her wing out every now and then. The little mice brought her worms and grubs from the fields to build up her strength.

Finally, one day, Blue Bird managed to stretch out her wing to its full extent. The time had come; she was ready to fly. The mice escorted her to the hole in the bottom of the barn door. She was a little nervous but she could see the sun shining brightly through the hole and hear the leaves rustling. She longed once again to be amongst their transparent greenness. So she cautiously squeezed her body through the hole.

The sun was so bright after the darkness of the barn that she had to half-close her eyes. The breeze ruffled her feathers and she could smell the sweetness of buttercups from the fields. The flowers were alive and dancing all around her. Her heart swelled and her outstretched wings responded to a gust of wind beneath them. All of a sudden, she was flying; she hadn't even thought about it, her wings were just greedy for the wind. She soared into the sky, whirling and diving, gliding and riding on the air. She gave herself over to the wind and its smells.

She did not notice the sun sinking behind the trees. She did not even notice that all the other birds had nestled down for the night. It wasn't until she felt the chill in the wind and saw the silvery light of the moon glistening on her feathers that she realised just how long she had been flying.

She swooped down to the barn and crept through the hole. She flew to the top beams and called to Mouse. Mouse appeared, wiping tears from her eyes with the end of her soft tail.

"I thought you had left without saying goodbye."

"Oh no, no. You have shown me the way to freedom and joy again," said Blue Bird. "The peace I felt in my heart was new to me – I felt it and it was real. l shall come back to see you and your family whenever I can and I will tell of your wondrous heart to every flower and bird that I see."

Blue Bird began to trill and the power of her throat filled the air with her own love and the love of her dear friend who had saved her.

Hungry Mouth

The Story Of Hungry Mouth Shows Us That:

- We can become stuck in negative behaviour/ addictions/relationships.

- Being stuck in any of these for too long a period, can have a negative effect on us – mentally, emotionally, physically and spiritually.

- Sometimes, when we are *stuck,* we become blind to our predicament and can't see a way out of it.

This Story Helps Us To:

Free ourselves from destructive addictions/ behaviour/relationships by facing the truth of our unhappy situation

Develop the courage, resources and abilities necessary to take positive action and free ourselves – however painful that may be

Find true happiness again.

Hungry Mouth

L eon lived in a small village at the bottom of a pleasant valley. The weather was beautiful and sunny there. The earth was fertile and provided for all the needs of the villagers. Like everyone else in the village, Leon lived a quiet life with all his friends around him. Leon and his friends loved the village but they often dreamt of leaving the safety of the valley and exploring the world beyond. One day, that opportunity arose for Leon and his friends.

The village elders called the group of young men to a meeting. It seemed that, many, many years ago during the Winter War, the village had had many of its precious artefacts stolen by the attacking hordes. The two sides had been at peace since long before Leon's birth and the villagers had accepted the loss of their precious artefacts. However, the Chief had just received word that they had been found in the Land of the Red Sky. It was a matter of great importance that these artefacts be restored to their rightful place in the village.

The Chief proposed that the young men should go and collect the artefacts and return them to the village. He understood that the Land of the Red Sky was very far away and it could take a year, maybe two years, to retrieve them. However, the boys would be provided for. They would be given enough money to carry them there and back by whatever means, allowing for every eventuality. The boys nearly bit the Chief's hand off in their eagerness to accept his offer. This was their chance at last to leave the village and with enough money for them to have plenty of adventures along the way. They set off immediately.

They had travelled for only a few months when they came across the mouth of a cave. It was towards evening and they were happily tired after the day's adventure. They crept into the mouth of the cave and, discovering that it was snug and warm, they felt safe and secure resting there for the night. They slept so soundly that they unanimously agreed the following morning that it was the best night's sleep they had since starting their journey. They gathered their belongings together and prepared to set off after breakfast.

However, when it came time for them to depart, Leon decided he did not want to leave the cave. At first, the other boys thought he was only jesting but they soon discovered that he was determined to stay in the cave.

"You will miss all the fun and adventure," they said. "This is the chance of our young lifetime and we do not want to waste it. The Chief has trusted you to come on this quest; we, too, have trusted you as our friend and companion."

Still Leon refused to leave the comfort of the dark cave.

"This is the most comfortable spot to stay in, the perfect place to sleep," Leon said.

"We came on this journey to have fun and see the world and collect the artefacts, not sleep in a dark cave all the time!" shouted Kevan, his closest friend.

"I have found total happiness and peace here, I am staying put. Nothing any of you can do or say will make me change my mind. It is my decision and I am staying," retorted Leon snappily.

The other young men became suspicious of the cave and felt that it would somehow steal their power and energy just to keep its dark mouth open. The thought of this gave them goose-pimples and made them shiver. They told Leon how they felt about the cave but still nothing could persuade him to leave it. Leon's friends walked slowly away, feeling both sad and angry with him. Leon entered the dark cave without even saying farewell to his close friends.

Leon's friends continued their happy wanderings around the world and had many wonderful experiences and adventures. They often talked about their friend Leon, asleep in the dark hungry cave, and indeed they shed some tears for him.

At first, Leon was very happy in his dark sleepy cave, which gave him great peace and comfort. Leon spent short periods of time each day, sitting on big rocks outside the cave, getting fresh air and taking in the view of this stony, arid land. As time went on, he began to spend more and more time in a twilight slumber in his dark cave and seldom ventured outside it.

Gradually, he became sleepier and sleepier; he began to have difficulty staying awake at all. He lost weight rapidly and became ghost-like and weak. Loneliness and fear began to creep into his heart, even in his sleep. The cave did not offer him the same peace and comfort any more. As time moved on, Leon found it hard even to stand up and walk. The cave showed no mercy whatsoever but sucked more and more of his energy and power from him.

In his drowsy twilight state, Leon kept telling himself that one day, one day, always one day, things would be different. He never fully understood what would be different. His mind was growing more tired and confused.

One night, Leon's Spirit broke through his slumber and spoke harshly to him. "Why are you trapping me in this dark lonely place? I demand to know," said his Spirit sternly.

"It is a good place," replied the drowsy, weary Leon.

"Well I hate it; it's smelly, empty, dark, lonely and full of fear. I'm afraid I can't stay here any more with you," his Spirit replied sadly.

"Oh, please don't leave me, Spirit, please don't go – don't go. If you go, I shall have nothing left – nothing, nothing," pleaded Leon.

"Leave the cave now," his Spirit commanded sternly.

"I am not able," whimpered Leon. "I am too weak."

"I shall breathe power into you but, once I do, you must flee quickly and not look behind you, no matter how difficult it is. Not even once must you stop and look behind you. If you look back, the cave will try to trick you and it will pull you back again, devouring your last bit of energy and power."

Crawling and stumbling, falling over, gashing his bare knees against the hard rocks, Leon managed to escape from the mouth of the cave. He did not look behind him, nor did he open his eyes to the burning sunlight, but kept on crawling forward in weakness and pain. The cave grumbled and roared and groaned and collapsed in upon itself. Still Leon did not look back.

"Open your eyes now," said his Spirit, "and stand up."

Leon opened his eyes, and in the warm glow of the morning sun, he saw walking towards him a young woman struggling to carry a child, a basket of fruit and a basket of eggs. She parked all three at Leon's feet.

"The child is too heavy to carry with the fruit and eggs," she said. "If you carry the eggs and fruit, I can carry the child easily. In return, I shall share the eggs and fruit with you."

Although in great pain and fear, Leon smiled for the first time since his friends had left. Gladly, he picked up the baskets of eggs and fruit and walked slowly and painfully alongside the woman and her child. Shortly, they came upon an oasis with green palm trees and lush grass. They sat down together, shared the food, collected ripe dates, took care of the child and spoke of many things.

The Fairy Whose Heart Was Stolen

The Story Of The Fairy Whose Heart Was Stolen Shows Us That:

- Childhood trauma and abuse can leave us deeply hurt and suffering on many levels.

- They can crush our sense of self and our confidence.

- Even as adults, they can trap us in childhood fear patterns.

- They can hinder us from making loving relationships with ourselves and others.

This Story Helps Us To:

Face our worst fears

Heal past childhood or adult trauma and abuse

Break out of loss, loneliness, isolation and deep sadness

Reclaim our power

Learn to love ourselves and develop loving relationships with others

The Fairy Whose Heart Was Stolen

Along time ago, in a faraway beautiful land, there was a very special, fairy glen named *The Glen of Promise*. A little fairy called Jamaerah lived with her mother and father in this glen. Her mother and father were very resourceful fairies and never minded helping others out. All other fairies loved Jamaerah. She was so beautiful to behold that all who saw her secretly longed for such beauty themselves. Her beautiful fairy green eyes shone like bright stars. Her grassy green curls tumbled around her gentle happy face. Jamaerah was a joyful little fairy and could be heard singing as she wandered around the fairy glen.

On her sixth birthday, when Jamaerah was happily tucked up in bed, her father took a long sharp knife out of the kitchen.

"What are you doing?" Jamaerah's mother asked, with an odd expression on her face.

"I am going to take some of Jamaerah's heart," he replied coldly.

"Do as you must," replied her mother with a shrug of her shoulders, "but don't tell me about it, I don't want to know."

When Jamaerah woke up, she was silent, frightened and tearful. Her parents smiled kindly at her and made a special breakfast. Her mother made a big pile of golden pancakes, smothered in golden syrup and butter, but Jamaerah could not eat the pancakes; she didn't feel hungry at all. Her father picked buttercups, her favourite flowers, and put them in a beautiful blue vase on the table. He smiled at Jamaerah and Jamaerah felt afraid.

Almost every night, that cold look would spread across Jamaerah's father's face and settle into his eyes. On these nights, he would go to the kitchen, get the big knife and quietly go into Jamaerah's room. At these times, Jamaerah's mother would then go into the kitchen herself and start to prepare a special meal for Jamaerah's breakfast. At first, Jamaerah felt terrified as the pieces of her heart were cut away and she mourned every moment for them. She lived in terror of the night-time when her father would come in with the knife.

Once, she dared to ask her father why he was cutting out her heart, piece by piece, and he told her that she was a very lucky lady not to have more than her heart cut out. She never asked him again because she knew by the look in his eyes that she had better not. She never asked her mother, as she was well aware that her mother knew about it because of the special breakfasts that would arrive each morning. She knew her mother didn't want her to ask.

Days went by, nights went by, and more and more of her heart was cut away. She grew empty inside and, finally, she felt nothing at all. Even her little limbs became numb and lost all their feeling. Each morning now, she could eat her mother's special breakfast because she didn't know whether she was hungry or not. She floated about, doing what a normal fairy girl would do, and nobody realised that her heart had been completely cut away. With her heart gone, her father didn't come with the knife any more. She didn't know how to act or what to do and had to be told by her mother and other fairies.

"Smile," her mother would say, and she would smile. She watched the other fairies and did what they did. She did everyone's bidding and didn't mind. She thought it was the right thing to do.

As she grew older and still looked so beautiful, different fairy boys would court her, laughing and playful with her in the long grass. Since she felt nothing, she would smile as they smiled and laugh as they laughed. When they said they didn't want to be with her any more, she smiled and said, "Thank You" and didn't feel anything.

One day, a fairy boy called Galgaliel somehow recognised that Jamaerah had no heart but he fell in love with her all the same. He was a beautiful fairy himself and told her he would help her find her heart. Jamaerah didn't care about her heart at all any more, she didn't even miss it. She just felt a cold, dark space where it had once been. All the same, she set off with Galgaliel in search of her heart.

They left the glen and went down into the swamps and, after nine days and nine nights of searching, they heard her heart faintly crying. The crying became louder and louder as they approached some bushes with the longest and sharpest thorns that Jamaerah had ever seen. Galgaliel approached the bushes but the heart retreated deeper and deeper into the bushes, crying louder. It became clear that only Jamaerah could rescue it because it belonged to her.

Jamaerah approached the bushes and a large angry snake with red eyes rose up, hissing in her face, and there were many smaller snakes behind it, hissing and trying to keep her away from the heart. For the first time since Jamaerah's heart was stolen, she felt terror.

"Jamaerah, Jamaerah, spit in the big snake's eyes!" shouted Galgaliel.

Terrified, Jamaerah spat as hard as she could right into the snake's red eyes. With a big bang that shook the trees for miles around, the snake exploded and fell to the ground in a pile of grey dust. All the smaller snakes dropped down to the ground and slithered away so that, in a few minutes, Jamaerah was standing all alone in the thicket and she could see her heart clearly through the thorns.

The heart was crying and studded with thorns, it was torn in places and there were little drops of blood glistening on the brambles. All of a sudden, Jamaerah felt a burning in the space where her heart had been, where it had once been dark and cold. She thought she could feel her heart beating again and she scrambled through the piercing thorns and snatched her heart from where it had been trapped. The heart immediately scurried into her chest, shaking Jamaerah's whole body as it did so.

Galgaliel pulled her back out of the bushes and she felt her whole body singing its way back to life. It was such a warm, intense, happy feeling. She felt that she might die then and there with happiness. Her whole body filled with love, which radiated out towards Galgaliel. But Galgaliel looked very sad and forlorn and said:

"I have to leave you now, dear, beautiful Jamaerah."

Jamaerah was dismayed and felt the deepest of sorrows in her heart and body as she watched him walk away through the swamp. Jamaerah turned and walked in the opposite direction, away from both Galgaliel and the glen.

She did not return to the glen for many years and, during those years, she nourished her heart with much joy, sorrow, pain, laughter, tears, despair and always a guiding ray of hope. Her heart grew strong and the wounds made by the knife and the thorns healed up, leaving only faint scars. Although Jamaerah felt at peace with her heart now, she still had no one to love. She used to visit the sea fairies often and, as she watched them frolicking together, she would often think of Galgaliel.

Jamaerah had a best friend in one of the sea fairies and, one day, she confessed her great desire to know the whereabouts of Galgaliel.

"Oh," said the sea fairy, "he was here many moons ago, and he came down into the deep sea with us. We trapped air in bubbles for him whilst he was in a dark cave looking for something. When we came back to the shore, he showed us what he had found. It was a piece of his heart that had been missing. He was so happy to have found it." Jamaerah felt great sadness and great joy at hearing this. She remembered how it had felt in the beginning to lose the pieces of her heart and she felt sad for him. She also remembered how it had felt when she had found her own heart and it had shaken her body.

She was recalling these feelings as she walked home along the beach in the moonlight. Suddenly, she saw a lone fairy shadow, out where the sea came to meet the rocks and sprayed itself upwards, glittering in the silvery blue light. Her heart jumped with recognition and she called out to Galgaliel. As she went to join him on the rocks, she realised that their hearts recognised each other in the way that only hearts that have been lost and found can.

For many moons, Jamaerah and Galgaliel lived among the rocks with great joy and peace. But after a while, both felt drawn back to the glen. Thus they set off together one morning, going back through the swamp and travelling for nine days and nine nights until they neared the glen.

Jamaerah and Galgaliel's parents were working together, gathering nettle leaves in the main clearing to make soup, so they were the first to see Jamaerah and Galgaliel returning to the glen. But a strange thing happened when they started towards their children. The four old fairies began to shake and to cover themselves with leaves. Jamaerah's father was in such a state, that he even fell over a big bumble-bee whilst trying to hide in some clover. The bee gave him a big nudge, knocking him over into Jamaerah's and Galgaliel's path.

The two beautiful young fairies were astonished: never before had they seen their parents behave in this way. They were stammering and sweating, creeping about on the ground. But whilst they looked down at their parents, who were by now covered in nettle stings because they had thrown down their tools and dived into the nettles in great haste, Jamaerah's and Galgaliel's restored hearts began to pulse harder and harder. They started to glow and strange whirring noises emanated from them. Even more curiously, the scars, which marked the places where the hearts had been cut out, began to glow brightly with such a dazzling light that their parents were forced to push their faces further into the stinging nettles to avoid being blinded.

Jamaerah and Galgaliel didn't know what to do. They could only stand and stare as their parents crawled around, howling, while the nettles stung their faces and their arms. And, as they watched, they realised that they were no longer afraid of their parents, that, really, they were quite pathetic, hiding in the nettles this way. Jamaerah even began to feel a little sorry for them. She looked round at Galgaliel and saw that a small smile was lifting the corners of his mouth and she felt one forming on her lips, too.

Their smiles got bigger and bigger until they broke into giggles, which gave way in turn to laughter that got louder and louder until the two beautiful fairies were crying with laughter. The tears streamed down their faces and, as they laughed, the noises and the light coming from their hearts gradually began to subside so that their parents could lift their faces out of the nettles and look up at these two beautiful laughing fairies.

Jamaerah and Galgaliel looked down again at the four swollen red faces staring at them and it made them laugh so much that their tears started to form little puddles around their parents. Gradually, they managed to stop laughing, and as they looked down at the puddles, they saw that their parents' tears of remorse and shame were dripping into the puddles as well. All at once, they were both overcome with sadness but also with love. They reached down together and helped their parents up out of the nettles.

The Ostriches

The Story Of The Ostriches Shows Us That:

- Often we sacrifice our health and happiness in the hope of being loved and accepted by others.

- We can be used and taken advantage of as a result, and even become ill.

- This will create inequality and resentment in our relationships.

- Hiding our real feelings and needs will hinder us in life.

This Story Helps Us To:

Resist the temptation to please other people at all costs

Form healthy relationships on a basis of equality with others

Identify our needs and accept help when offered

Let go of hurt and grief

Learn and grow strong

The Ostriches

It was a long, scorching hot summer and, during this time, the rivers dried up to a trickle and most of the lakes dried up altogether. Only the largest lakes managed to retain some water to provide a sanctuary for the frogs and little mudfish but even these were reduced to mere water-holes. A vicious crocodile kept guard over one such water-hole and he grabbed and ate many animals that came to drink there. The animals were terrified to drink from this water-hole but there was little else on offer in this parched and burning hot land. Of necessity, they were forced to take a deadly risk at the water-hole every night to quench their burning thirst.

One night, a flock of Ostriches waited for their chance to drink at the water-hole. A female Ostrich, named Ezzie, took the first turn at the water's edge to protect the other Ostriches and give them a better chance of survival. That night, they all drank and managed to escape without harm. Ezzie was universally acclaimed for her generous spirit in going first to the water-hole. The next night, they did the same thing, Ezzie going first to make it safer for the others. But one night, just as they bent their heads down to drink, a loud voice boomed out from the deep water.

"I won't eat any of you Ostriches if each of you gives me one of your feathers every night. There are fifteen of you and I will have fifteen feathers every night. I want to make a feather-bed for my lady love."

The Ostriches trembled in fear but all lined up around the water-hole and the crocodile yanked one big feather out of each bird's flesh. They winced and cringed in pain as the feathers were ripped from them. The crocodile let out a big holler of glee and bared his menacing, razor-sharp teeth.

The next morning, the Ostriches sat together, complaining to each other about their pain and worrying about having to give a feather every night.

"I shall go on my own," said Ezzie.

"But Vicious Jaws needs fifteen feathers and you can only give one," replied a female Ostrich.

"Don't worry," she told the others, "I shall give him fifteen of my own feathers tonight, one for each of you."

They all voiced their gratitude to her.

"You are the very best," they said, "thank you so much." They gave her many pecks and kisses.

"It's nothing," she said, "what are a few feathers?"

Each night, Ezzie presented herself to be plucked of fifteen feathers by Vicious Jaws. During her ordeal, the rest of the Ostriches drank safely from the water-hole to their heart's content. Ezzie's Ostrich friends got so used to her sacrificing herself on their behalf that they even forgot to thank her at times. Their ungratefulness made Ezzie very sad – and angry, too – but she never complained about it. The nights when they remembered to show their gratitude, she was very happy indeed.

One night, when Ezzie was too ill to have all fifteen of her feathers plucked, the other Ostriches voiced their disappointment in her. How could she not sacrifice herself for them on this occasion!

Ezzie vowed to try harder next time even though her flesh was torn and bleeding. Indeed, she did try harder and managed to give up her feathers in future so that the other Ostriches could be spared.

When the crocodile had enough feathers to build his feather-bed he told Ezzie she didn't have to give any more. Ezzie's heart sank when she heard the news but she couldn't figure out why. Having feathers ripped out by the crocodile was a painful business and she didn't have many more feathers to give. Indeed, she was almost bald.

The other Ostriches kept out of her way from then on and seemed a bit embarrassed by her quaint bald looks and blood-streaked flesh. It was the mating season among the Ostriches and not even one male Ostrich gave her a second glance. Ezzie's heart felt crushed, broken and abandoned and she became very ill. The hot sun scorched and ate into her bare skin, leaving big red blisters that soon turned into running sores.

"After all I have given, no one cares about me now," she sobbed desolately to herself. She tried to drag herself to the water-hole but was too weak and ill to reach it. Her throat was now parched and her eyes were bleeding from the burning sun.

A passing Warthog with large tusks and ever-watchful eyes spotted Ezzie lying there alone and helpless on the burning scorched earth. He came over to sniff her since he was curious and had never seen such a featherless blistered Ostrich before.

After sniffing her, he became very concerned. "My dear, you are burning up and ill," he said. There was gentleness in his voice. "Would you like me to take you back to my family so that you can grow strong again? We are without hair or feathers ourselves and know how to keep cool and well."

Even in her weak state, she wanted to say "No" she'd manage fine on her own. But, just for once, something different happened. She said, "Yes, I would like that very much." Without further ado, the Warthog hoisted Ezzie onto his back and hastened home with her.

Back at the Warthog's den in its cool, dripping cavern, Ezzie was protected from the burning sun and given food and water. In the cool of the evenings, the young pigs taught her how to forage for food. She had never had it so good. There was such a variety of roots and seeds that she had never tasted or known about before. She quickly grew healthy and strong and, soon, beautiful shiny feathers began to grow on her. She played with the pigs and showed them all the games and dances she knew. The Warthogs were so proud and happy to be her friend and taught her many exciting new things in return.

As soon as Ezzie's feathers had all grown back, she went back to see the Ostrich clan. She walked among them with her head held high. When a young bossy male Ostrich tried to woo her, she just shook her head and said:

"I know that you are not the one for me, dear."

When some of the Ostriches asked her for some nesting feathers, she replied:

"Now you had better use your own, dear. Whatever gave you the idea that I would give you feathers when you have got plenty of your own?"

Ezzie settled back in amongst her flock of Ostriches but she never forgot the lessons she had learned. In the scarce, arid times, all the Ostriches shared equally the responsibility of going first to the water-hole.

Ezzie lived very happily with her fellow Ostriches to the end of her days. She never forgot her friends the Warthogs and went back to see them regularly.

The Blue Fairies & The Power Stone

The Story Of The Blue Fairies & The Power Stone Shows Us That:

- If we lose the ability to speak up for ourselves, we shall then lose confidence and feel powerless against bullying and cruelty.

- We may become depressed/anxious/ill.

- We may try to placate/please others in the false hope of winning favour.

This Story Helps Us To:

Break free from the negative grip of others and reclaim our power

Be open to accepting help and guidance

Take courage; speak up for ourselves, even if we are afraid

Help others speak up for themselves, too

The Blue Fairies & The Power Stone

The Blue Fairies lived in the heart of the Blue Mountain, where they had lived since the earth began. They were peaceful Fairies, small, with bright, sparkling, dancing blue eyes and blue hair; in fact, they were blue all over. They had great vision. They could fly way up into the heavens through the clouds and mist. The burning sun never scorched or harmed them. Some even claimed that they could see the Great Goddess and were her special ever-present companions. Others said they were angels because they could bridge all the different worlds. They were friendly, brave little Fairies with hope and love in their hearts. They lived peacefully with their neighbours, the Green and Pink Fairies, and offered a helping hand to them whenever they could.

The warlike, greedy Red and Black Fairies came from far across the sea. They resented other Fairies and took pleasure in terrifying and torturing them. They had ugly, angry, bulging red and black burning coal-like eyes. At night they would leave their home and fly to the Blue Mountain – the home of the Blue Fairies. Here they cast wicked spells and skulked around looking for Blue Fairy children to steal.

One stormy night, as the wind moaned and blustered and the rain beat down unmercifully, they crept into the home of the Blue Fairies. They cast an evil spell and stole a beautiful Blue Fairy child called Orla. When the Blue Fairies realised that little Orla had been taken from them, they were heartbroken and had no idea where their little Orla had gone to. The Red and Black Fairies had cast a spell so strong that they could not be seen.

The little Blue Fairy child, Orla, was taken "far across the sea" to the land of the Red and Black Fairies. Their home was in the lower regions of the earth, and this is where Orla was taken to as their slave. They stole her magic powers from her – her flight magic, her joy, her peace and, worst of all, her special vision. She was terrified, fearful, and constantly anticipating new calamities. She felt very guilty because these bad Fairies had stolen her from her family; she knew her family would be crying and worrying about her. She didn't want her family to be crying and worrying about her; she just wanted them to be happy the way they used to be.

Orla felt trapped and suffocated in the Red and Black Fairies' dark cavernous chambers. She shed bitter tears and begged to go home. They just laughed at her and made her slave harder for them. She had to wash, cook and clean for the Red and Black Fairies while they took delight in finding new ways to torture her.

Little Orla grew more silent with each passing day until finally she didn't talk any more. She didn't even shed any more tears. She just tried to do the bidding of the Red and Black Fairies as best she could. She felt that being silent and dedicated was the best way for her to stay alive.

Gradually, her once bright blue eyes became dull and sore. Her little hands trembled and her tiny bones ached. She worked so hard and did everything right just to please the Red and Black Ones. Alone in the dark, she often imagined her family back home but dared not think about them too much in case her heart broke beyond repair.

One night, as she lay silent and all alone in a corner of the damp cavern, she was amazed to hear a gentle voice calling to her. It came from a small blue Stone:

"Hello, little Blue Fairy Orla," said the Stone, "you may not know it but I am a Power Stone and I can help you. I can awaken the courage and power hidden within you. This ability was given to me long ago when the earth was new and I have guarded this precious gift ever since. I want to be your friend. Don't be afraid of me, Little One, I want to help you."

In a trembling whisper, Orla told the Power Stone her sad story, with her little head cocked to one side and salty tears falling like rain down her cheeks.

"Listen to me carefully now for I know a way out of here," said the Power Stone.

"I *can't* get out of here," said Orla, "they will catch me and kill me. I can't sneak out."

"No, you can't sneak out," said the Power Stone, "and you don't have to. You will only get out if you raise your voice and speak up loudly for yourself."

Now little Orla grew suspicious and thought that the Stone was trying to trick her.

"Oh Fairy Orla, I didn't mean to alarm you," said the Power Stone, "I am not your enemy, I am your friend. You, little Fairy, have to understand that the Red and Black Fairies are only frightened of one thing and that is a raised voice. Once they hear a raised voice, they tremble with fear and put their fingers in their ears to block it out. If you raise your voice and speak up for yourself, the strong spell they have laid on you will be broken forever. They will be so frightened that they will want to get rid of you right away."

"But little Power Stone," Orla protested, "I *never* speak loudly, none of us Blue Fairies is able to do that. I don't think we Fairies have ever spoken up loudly for ourselves."

"Ah, so sad, so sad," said the Power Stone. "I can help you, though, Orla. I can flash energy voice into you so that you *will* be able to speak up loudly for yourself."

"I would like to try," said Orla, "but I am very afraid."

"Go on, even if you are afraid, what have you to lose?" encouraged the Power Stone.

"What shall I shout?" asked Orla.

"What would you like to shout?" asked the Power Stone.

"I would like to shout, 'I want to get out of here right now and go home, you are all mean and nasty here!'

"Then take me in your hand and shout!" ordered the Stone.

Little Orla did just that and her voice was loud and clear when she spoke up: she surprised herself and even smiled and giggled.

"That was good," beamed the Power Stone. "Do it again, Orla."

As they were practising, the Red and Black Fairies returned home from their feast. One would think they had come from a funeral, not a feast, so grumpy did they appear. Little Fairy Orla, with the Power Stone in her pocket, ran towards them and let out a piercing, loud scream:

"I want to get out of here and go home! I am not afraid of you any more!"

The scream shook the very foundations of the Red and Black Fairies home. The Red and Black Fairies became paralysed with fear. They stuck their fingers in their ears and crouched on the ground, their trembling bottoms in the air. Little Blue Fairy Orla, with the Power Stone in her pocket, gave each of their raised bottoms a little kick as she ran from the lower regions into the sun-bright morning. She heard the Power Stone chuckling in her pocket.

A remarkable thing happened once Orla was out in the bright sunlight. She got all her gifts back. She was able to see again, even into other worlds. She was able to fly again and she felt great joy in her heart. Her little work-torn hands became perfect and shining again. The Black and Red Fairy spell had been completely broken; she could see her home and her family again. She flew all the way back to her own Blue Fairies with the Power Stone in her pocket.

The members of her Fairy Family were overjoyed to see their beautiful Fairy Child Orla again. They dried their big tears and combed their long blue hair for the first time since her departure. Orla told them of her ordeal and her escape with the Power Stone's help. Together with the Power Stone, Orla taught all her family about the gift of being able to raise your voice and speak up for yourself.

When all the Blue Fairies had learned how to raise their voices and speak up for themselves, each one received as a present beautiful specks of gold in their hair as well as the gift of courage and song. From that day to this, the Power Stone continues to be honoured and guarded by all the Blue Fairies.

The Princess
Of Sleep

The Story Of The Princess Of Sleep Shows Us That:

- We can become too obsessed with what we haven't got and miss out on the wonderful things we already have.

- This can open us up to jealousy, resentment and bitterness

- It prevents us from relating lovingly to others around us

- We miss out if we fail to appreciate the present moment

This Story Helps Us To:

Live in the present moment and appreciate all we already have.

Face up to our negative feelings, overcoming greed, prejudice, jealousy, bitterness and resentment.

Develop an open, loving heart.

Story Of The Princess Of Sleep

There once was a beautiful Princess who lived in a magnificent palace with her mother the Queen and her father the King. She was the Treasure of their hearts and they showered her with great love and the petals of affection. The Princess's eyes were as blue as the cornflowers in the meadows and her cheeks were like soft pink roses. Golden silken hair fell in curls down her back. Indeed, she was so beautiful to behold that all who saw her were enchanted with her grace and beauty.

However, all was not well with the little Princess. In the silence of the night there was a dark shadow moving towards her heart.

One day, while she was sitting alone in the royal garden, a fairy appeared before her. The fairy held in her hand a golden wand that sparkled in the sunlight. Her star-like eyes danced and twinkled, casting rays of spinning light, silver and gold, around the Princess.

"How are you, beautiful little Princess?" asked the fairy. Why are you sitting here all alone?"

"I want to be alone!" shouted the little Princess in anger. "There is no reason why I, who am a Princess, should have to play with stupid servant children."

"I want to be a Queen right now." She pouted and her voice became harsh and shrill. "I want to ride the royal horses. I want to command the servants and the slaves. I want to sit on the jewelled throne and see people bow before me. I want to marry a beautiful prince, who will be majestic and noble, and I shall be the Queen of his heart and rule the Kingdom with him."

The fairy was startled and dismayed to hear such words. Her starry eyes grew misty and a diamond-bright tear trickled down her cheek.

"Why, little Princess, you are but a child," said the fairy. "You have the brightest rays of the sun and moon in your heart now. They will shine so brightly if you let them and will melt away the dark shadow that is growing around your heart. Be a child now, beautiful Princess, and when the time is right for you, you will indeed be Queen." The Princess's beautiful corn flower-blue eyes grew dark and distant on hearing the fairy's words. Her rosy lips pouted sourly.

"Put me to sleep, put me to sleep, fairy," demanded the Princess. "Put me to sleep for ten years. When I wake up, I shall be old enough to marry a prince, who will one day be King, while I shall be the Queen of the Kingdom." The fairy was dismayed but did as she was told. She touched the little Princess with her magic wand and the little Princess fell into the deepest sleep.

The King and Queen and all their subjects mourned for the little Princess. The palace became silent and an air of grief like a wet grey blanket hung heavy over it. In the courtyard the royal pets slumbered, the clocks ceased ticking and the spiders stopped spinning. The King and Queen became very sorrowful and forlorn but took comfort from the knowledge that, one day, their beautiful Princess would wake up again.

Many moons and day-breaks came and went. Days and nights silently slipped by and finally, when ten years had passed, the Princess moaned and roused herself from her slumber. She was a beautiful woman Princess now, radiant and full of summer promise. There was much rejoicing and the King and Queen wept with happiness. The strain imposed by years of sorrow and pain drained from their noble faces. The whole palace sang of the awoken Princess's presence and beauty. In the courtyard the royal pets awoke and the dogs barked, the clocks began ticking again and the spiders once more began spinning and weaving.

"Where is the Prince, strong, noble and handsome, who will marry me now and make me Queen?" demanded the Princess as she entered the royal court. On hearing those words, a new light of hope shone in the eyes of the King and Queen. The most revered noble prince in all the land was summoned to the palace by the King. He was indeed handsome to behold and when the Princess saw him, she smiled warmly and her heart leaped for joy.

The handsome Prince stood tall and proud before the Princess. She waited for him to ask for her hand in marriage. He looked troubled and thoughtful and said nothing for a while. A salty tear fell down his cheek. "I cannot marry you, dear Princess," he said. "I cannot marry you for I love another, whose eyes shine with the light of the sun and the light of the moon and whose heart has learned to play with the stars. She is the one whom I shall marry and stay with for the rest of my time in this land."

The Princess became dejected and angry. Her eyes grew dark and distant. She hastened to talk to her father.

"Father," she said, "if I do not marry and if you and my mother the Queen get too old to reign, shall I be Queen then?"

"Of course you shall, my dear little Princess," her father replied. "You are of royal blood and our only child, all we have will be yours and you will indeed be Queen one day. However, it will be many years before we are too old to reign, my dear Princess, enjoy these years. So much laughter and love are here for you now, do not let them pass you by."

The Princess shrugged her shoulders and hastily made her way back to the royal garden, where she sat down alone on the royal rocking-chair.

Her corn flower-blue eyes grew cold, hard and dim; her lovely pink cheeks flushed crimson.

The shadow around her heart grew darker and bigger.

"Fairy, fairy!" she called out loudly, "Come to me now, right now!"

The fairy appeared before her once again.

"And how are you, Princess?" enquired the fairy in a very gentle voice. "The most proud, strong, handsome Prince in all the land has refused to marry me, he loves another less fair than I," retorted the Princess sharply.

"O beautiful Princess," said the fairy, "there are many strong, handsome princes in the land who will be honoured to marry you. He is not the only one."

Looking cold and sullen, the Princess replied, "He is the one I want to marry, he is the one I want to reign as King while I am his Queen."

"Put me to sleep for ten more years; put me to sleep."

The fairy looked very sad on hearing these words again. She did as she was bidden and put the Princess to sleep for another ten years.

The King and Queen were dismayed when they found the Princess asleep again. Sorrow and pain once more stole into their hearts and took away their joy. The years came and went and, with each passing year, the King and Queen grew older and sadder. They could no longer reign and remained in the palace, cared for by the strongest, most handsome Prince who was, by appointment, the new King. The old King and Queen were loved dearly and showered with kindness by both him and his Queen, the one whose eyes shone with the light of the sun and the moon and whose heart played with the stars.

After ten long years, the sleeping Princess woke up and discovered that her parents, the King and Queen were old, weak and frail with sorrow and no longer reigned over the Kingdom. She wept bitter tears now that she could not be Queen because her chance had been given to someone else.

She fled the palace and the eyes of her parents and ran once more to the royal garden.

"Fairy!" she cried, "Help me! Come and help me, I don't know what to do. My beauty is fading; my father and mother are frail and ill. I can no longer be Queen. What shall I do? Please help me."

"I shall help you," said the fairy.

"You have given me your spring years,

You have given me your summer years,

You have even given me your autumn years.

You cannot get them back."

"They are in my fairy world where spring, summer, and autumn dance together. Princess, I can but give you a magic violet key to make each day *new* again and I can send a violet sunbeam into your heart to drive away the dark shadow. I can only give you these things if you wish them."

The fairy's eyes were sad and pleading as she gazed intently at the Princess.

"I wish them," said the Princess, "I wish them so."

"Please give me this, my final wish, dear fairy."

The fairy touched the Princess with her magic wand. A violet sunbeam pierced the Princess's heart.

The dark shadow around it came rushing out of the Princess's chest and disappeared into the earth.

With her magic, glowing, violet key, the Princess was now able to open the closed doors in her heart. The Princess smiled for the first time in many years and her eyes shone bright with the light of dawn, the magic of the day, the secrets of dusk and the mysteries of the night. She saw all things new again and she now knew that sunbeams danced in her heart. She thanked the fairy and ran to tell her ever-loving parents of her new-found joy.

She became good friends with the new King and Queen and cared for her parents with such love and warmth that they regained their sparkle and, many said, looked ten years younger. She fell in love with the new King's cousin, who was a carpenter at the palace. They were married shortly afterwards and spent many hours walking in the royal garden and tending to the flowers. Together, they would greet the dawn, the daylight hours, and the secret nights with great joy and happiness.

The Quails
And Snake

The Story Of The Quails And Snake Shows Us That:

- Tending to think the worst can make us unduly anxious and frightened.

- We can become stuck in this type of thinking and fail to see an obvious way out of our dilemma.

- Fear and anxiety can make us ill, hopeless, depressed and "go around in circles."

This Story Helps Us To:

Recognise that our fears are not always based on truth and we need to look at the reality of the situation

Do the right thing despite our fear and anxiety

Learn from our experiences and mistakes, and develop more balanced views

The Quails And Snake

W hile a flock of Quails was engrossed in eating the juicy, delicious, purple-red berries that lay in abundance under a mulberry tree, Snake, who lived in a hole in the tree trunk, secretly watched them. Snake saw the gentle Quails hopping around joyfully and playfully while feasting on the mulberries.

It maddened Snake that the Quails were so happy. He himself was feeling bored and grumpy and wanted a bit of entertainment. He decided to terrify the Quails for his own amusement and pleasure. "Stupid-looking birds," he muttered to himself, "I shall teach you how to tremble before me; I shall steal the happiness out of your hearts." He slithered his scaly head and half his body out of his nest, startling the Quails. In a threatening and authoritative voice he declared:

"You have to stay here and grow fat; you are going to be my dinner. I cannot eat you now, you are too thin and scrawny. Grow fat, grow fat quickly!" he screamed. "I am getting hungrier and hungrier!"

While he spoke, the Quails saw his head puff up dangerously and his flicking tongue dart about fiercely. He opened his jaws wide, displaying four big dangerous-looking fangs. Snake hissed loudly and cast a pall of fear over the Quails. He then slithered silently and with deliberate slowness back into his hole.

The Quails trembled and felt overwhelmed with fear. They became frantic and cried out to each other:

"Oh, oh, oh, Snake is going to get us, Snake is going to get us! We are doomed, we are doomed; we had better eat quickly, Snake is going to kill us, he ordered us to eat quickly and grow fat for him, oh, oh, Snake is going to kill us and eat us! "

The beautiful mulberries that had enchanted the Quails moments before became part of their nightmarish fears. Frantically, the Quails started to eat the mulberries. Their fear intensified with every berry they ate. Fear set off bad diarrhoea in many of them. Some of them became so ill with terror that they could not eat at all. Some of them jumped around not knowing which mulberries to eat. Some of them felt sick and vomited the mulberries. As the days passed, they became more frantic and fearful. All grew thinner and thinner.

Snake watched from his secret nest in the tree, pleased with the power he had over the Quails. He cackled with laughter and puffed himself up with pride. He laughed so much that his old head wobbled uncontrollably up and down. He hadn't known it would go so well.

On one dark night, when the Quails were at their lowest ebb, the spirit of one little Quail woke up from slumber and spoke to them. "You can fly, snake can't fly" she said. "All you little Quails know how to fly; you have just forgotten that you can. Fly away now and be free, quickly, fly, fly away!"

"Yes, yes, yes!" they all managed to cry out together. Flapping their wings uncertainly, they all took to the air. They did not stop until they had landed on the side of their own familiar mountain. Although exhausted, their hearts were filled with joy because they were free from Snake's power over them.

Their friends welcomed them home and they feasted together on the choicest grains and berries. The Quails told their friends of their ordeal and all vowed never to be tricked by Snake or anyone else again. They taught the lesson so painfully learned to their children and to their children's children.

The Sad Giant

The Story Of The Sad Giant Shows Us That:

- We can harden our hearts towards others, treat them badly, rationalise our hostility so that it appears justified.

- We can be too influenced by superficial appearances.

- We can cause great grief and distress to others by treating them unjustly.

- We can be blind to truth and beauty when they are there before our eyes.

This Story Helps Us To:

Overcome our fears and prejudice

See truth and beauty where they lie hidden

Develop courage and bravery, honesty and justice

Become open-minded and open-hearted

Use the power of love to transform ourselves and our relationships

---

The Sad Giant

An ugly Giant lived in the village known as The Heart of Stone and he was just about as ugly as any Giant could be. He was covered in big horny growths and warts. His nose was like the snout of a pig and his mouth as wide as any horse's mouth could be. His red and purple ears stuck out like big heads of cabbage and his outsize head swayed about as if it were trying to balance on his body. He rarely spoke and when he did, his booming voice trembled and broke.

No one ever hung about to hear what the ugly Giant had to say; instead, people stuck their fingers in their ears and scurried off so fearsome was his voice. People whispered to each other that they felt their village was cursed and blackened by having such an ugly wicked monster living among them.

The sad Giant hid away in the daytime as much as he could. When he got too lonely, he would wander about the village forlornly hoping someone would offer him a kind word or a smile. No one ever did. Whenever he heard children crying, he too would begin to sob and cover his face with his big awkward hands. He never wanted anyone to see him crying, but if one looked carefully, his enormous shoulders could be seen heaving with the sobs.

The villagers called a meeting to discuss how they could get rid of the Giant. The parson was invited as the main speaker and he entered the meeting hall with much pomp and ceremony. He was dressed in a long black robe and had a determined look on his round, plump, red face. His eyes bulged with excited aggression and his loud voice was harsh and accusing.

"We must banish the Giant from our village, we must banish him right away before it is too late and we are ripped apart by him!" shouted the parson, pumping his fists up and down in the air. His audience took up the frenzied cry:

"Banish the Giant, banish the Giant, banish the Giant!" they all shouted.

"Who will tell the Giant?" asked the parson more quietly looking pointedly in the direction of the big men-folk.

No one replied to the parson's question at first because no one had the courage to tell the Giant to leave the village. They hoped that someone else would do it.

"I am scared," said one man, "he will kill me."

"I am scared, he will eat me," said another.

"I am scared that he will eat my children," said yet another.

And so it went on – each man with his own fears and excuses.

The clear voice of a young lady quieted the protesting villagers into stunned silence.

"I shall do it," said a young lady named Avellino, as she manoeuvred her wheelchair up to the front and faced the people. Her long red hair framed her elfin freckled face and her big blue eyes shone brightly. "I shall tell the Giant that he is not wanted or welcome in his own village," she announced. Avellino had no legs and her family could not afford artificial legs for her.

"He will eat you!" they all cried with one voice, "he will eat you!"

"It is highly dangerous," warned the parson, wagging a finger at her.

"He will snap your head in two!" bellowed a fat man as he advanced towards Avellino, pointing his finger at her.

"I have no fear of the Giant. Why should I fear such a gentle Giant?" Avellino replied with confidence.

An awkward silence hung in the air for some time. The people stared hard at Avellino. There was a look of confusion and bewilderment on their faces. Eventually, the parson spluttered out that Avellino had least to lose, as she had no legs.

Avellino's father, who stood at the back of the hall, rushed forward and gave the parson a poke on the nose, knocking him to the ground, where he lay squealing for some time with his legs in the air.

"My daughter," bellowed the father, "is as good as any of you, even if she does have no legs!"

Avellino's father believed that the Giant was indeed harmless but he had not the courage to speak up on his behalf. He secretly admired his daughter for her bravery in agreeing to talk to the Giant. Eventually, it was unanimously agreed that they should call the Giant to the meeting and Avellino should tell him of the villagers' decision.

The Giant lumbered in with faltering steps and his head bobbing about from side to side. He was led before Avellino. In a very earnest voice, she told the Giant that the people wanted him to leave the village. She told him that they wanted him to leave right away because he would never be welcome in the village. She said they hated him living in their village and believed he was wicked and evil.

The Giant held his head high but his heart felt as though crushed by a gigantic rock. He felt the life drain out of him and thought he was going to die on the spot. He wanted to roar, he wanted to run, he wanted to resist but he knew that, if he resisted, he would be hunted down and driven away. He stood silent for some time as if he were rooted to the spot and the only movement visible was his big upturned head swaying about, trying to find a resting-place on his neck.

"What shall I do all alone, hidden away, seeing no children playing, with no one in sight? I shall be all alone. I shall shrivel up, I shall die and they won't even bury my body," he thought to himself. He was truly crushed and broken and tried hard not to show it.

"I shall go," he said aloud and his voice boomed out but with a quiver in it that made people uneasy. His whole body trembled and shook with the effort of speaking.

"Mr Giant, wait a minute!" shouted Avellino. "You will not leave on your own. I am going with you."

The villagers were struck dumb. Had the lady lost her mind, they wondered? Her father looked at her, perplexed, but she just smiled up at him.

"Who will look after you?" demanded her family and the villagers.

"The Giant will, of course," she said.

The Giant could not believe what he was hearing. The pieces of his shattered heart began to mould together and vibrate, to sing and whistle. The air took up the notes and created music that only the Giant and Avellino could hear. A smile like a bright sun lit up the Giant's face. The dumbfounded villagers, including the parson, scuttled home without a word to each other. Avellino left the village with the Giant, promising her family that she would be back to see them in a few moon's time.

True to her word, the Giant and Avellino reappeared in the village. All the villagers gathered round them in the meeting hall. They were amazed that she was alive, well and healthy. But they were also secretly dismayed because it proved that the Giant was not as evil as they believed he was, and this they could not accept with good grace. So all the villagers then promised Avellino that they would contribute to artificial legs for her if she would but stay in the village. They even begged her to stay, saying they missed her and warning her that the Giant could turn evil at any moment. They asked only for a small token in return for the great gift they offered. They made what they considered a meagre request: just that she would once more ask the Giant to leave the village forever, for their safety and for hers.

Avellino agreed and the villagers were delighted. But once more the Giant's heart was quivering in pain. All were silent, including the Giant, whose head was bowed low while his body trembled slightly. Avellino sat up very straight in her chair and spoke very clearly and loudly to the gathered people. This is what she said:

"I don't care about the artificial legs. If you give them to me freely, without making such a cruel demand, I shall be grateful. If you don't, so be it. I shall not betray and reject the one I love for a pair of artificial legs. I love the Giant and when he goes from the village at your request, I shall go with him."

The Giant came close to Avellino and let out an almighty roar that shook the meeting hall. He stood in front of Avellino and asked her to say those words again. Avellino roared the words and her voice was almost as strong as the Giant's:

"I love the Giant!" She looked up into the Giant's face and smiled.

The crowd was dismayed and enraged. A wave of fear swept silently through the crowd.

The Giant let out another almighty roar and crashed down to the ground, causing it to tremble and shake. A very strange thing happened then.

The Giant's nose fell off and was absorbed into the earth like a puddle of rain. White steam began to hiss from the fallen Giant. His whole body split in two, it groaned and roared. A young man stepped out of the broken body of the Giant. He was tall and handsome and his warm smile lit up the hall. He lifted the young woman from her wheelchair and held her in his strong arms.

"I am a magic Prince with magic powers from the Land of Love and Truth and my name is Netzach, which means victory," declared the young man. He continued:

"An evil curse was put on me by a cruel enemy of our land. Many of my people were killed and I was banished. I was offered a choice between death or assuming the form of an Ugly Giant. I chose the latter in the hope that one day I would bring justice to my people by breaking the curse, a curse that only love could break. Now that it is broken, my enemies will fight and destroy each other and have no more power to destroy and kill my people. My beautiful Princess here has seen beyond the veil of illusion and, in giving true love to me, she has broken the evil curse."

Avellino was so happy that she thought it could not be true – she must be dreaming.

"Now that I have reclaimed my lost magic," the prince declared, "I want to use my magic power to heal my Princess's legs."

He lifted his face up to the sky and a shower of light fell around him and Avellino. The light was so bright that no one dared to look at it. When the light disappeared, Avellino was seen *standing* beside her Prince. Tears of joy fell down her beautiful face as she walked back and forth on her perfect legs.

A week later, they were married and Prince Netzach changed the name of the village from Heart of Stone to Heart of Love. The people of the village had learned a lesson they would never forget.

The Shadow

The Story Of The Shadow Shows Us That:

- We can become stuck in *a negative mind-set,* which will make us miserable and depressed.

- This mind-set blinds us to the wonders around us.

- Holding onto a *pessimistic mind-set* will make others want to avoid us at all costs.

This Story Helps Us To:

Recognise when we are stuck in a persistently negative way of thinking

Take the action necessary to free ourselves

Appreciate the good things we have in life

Develop a more positive outlook and bring joy and playfulness into our hearts

The Shadow

S holdan lived in a small house on the edge of a village in a beautiful valley, with a clear sparkling stream running through it from the surrounding mountains. Like all the others who lived in this village, he had everything his heart could desire.

Sholdan was a handsome young man. He was well-built with good features, a mop of raven-black hair and brown, soulful eyes. His handsome face, though, was marred by his gloomy expression. His eyebrows pulled into a frown and his mouth drooped a bit and was tense and tight. His face looked like that of a man suffering hardship.

Sholdan was not a happy man. There was something quite unusual about Sholdan. He slept in bed all day, saying it was too late to get up, anyway. He couldn't sleep at night, saying it was a hard life for a man who couldn't sleep. When the sun shone brightly, he said it was too bright. When the rain fell, he said it rained too much. When the wind blew, he said he got tired of its whistle. When the great trees spread out their leaves and created shade to sit in, he said the shady area was too big. Under the smaller trees, he said their shady area was too small. When he heard children play, he said they got on his nerves. When they were silent, he said it was too quiet. When the other young men and women went dancing and frolicking, he said they didn't pay him enough attention. When they did pay him attention, he said it was too much.

Sholdan finally decided that he had an incurable malady and was doomed to a life of pain. He took to plodding along slowly. His gait grew stiff and his back began to bend. He wanted to know why he had been chosen to suffer such an affliction. After much consideration, he decided to visit the Wise Master for some answers. The Master lived on top of the mountain so Sholdan begrudgingly got up a little earlier than usual so that he could complete his journey within a day. When he reached the top of the mountain, he saw the Master sitting with his eyes closed, enjoying the beautiful day. As Sholdan approached, he opened one of his eyes.

"How can I be of help?" the Master asked.

Sholdan began to tell the Master about his incurable affliction. He related tale of woe after tale of woe to the silent Master. Eventually, Sholdan was startled into silence by the loud snoring of the Master.

Sholdan was alarmed and wondered if perhaps he should do something but then he decided he didn't know what to do. The Master finally opened his eyes and Sholdan started to tell him about his debilitating affliction all over again. This time the Master lay down and snored even more loudly. When he woke up, Sholdan was sitting near him with a look of consternation on his face. The Master shook his head slowly.

"This is the hardest day I have had in a long time," said the Master out loud to himself.

"What was so hard, Master?" enquired the mournful Sholdan.

"You," said the Master, "your affliction is so serious, it made me fall asleep."

"Is there any hope for me, Master?"

"Oh, there is indeed."

"What is it?" asked Sholdan, expecting some great wisdom.

"Get off this mountain as quickly as you can for both our sakes," replied the Master, "and look towards the children for only they can give you the answer."

"But I hate children," retorted Sholdan sourly, "I hate them, they are so boring and loud and frivolous."

"That's a good sign," said the Master and he closed his eyes and started to snore again. Sholdan became resentful and angry with the Master. The Master was supposed to have great wisdom and yet he was saying such stupid, irrational things. Perhaps he was a stupid man, after all.

Without even saying farewell to the Master, Sholdan made his way slowly down the mountain, feeling dispirited and bored. When he reached the foot of the mountain, he heard children calling out to each other and laughing with great gusto. The children were racing around, trying to catch each other's shadows. Some of them rushed over to meet him.

"*Run quickly, quickly*," they called out to him, "and we shall try to catch your shadow."

Without thinking, Sholdan broke into a run, with the screaming, laughing children in hot pursuit. He ducked this way and that, turning and twisting and leaping away from small outstretched hands. Finally, some of the hands grabbed him and held him tight whilst the other children jumped onto his shadow. The shadow screeched and squirmed and kicked.

"Please, please," begged Sholdan, "get off my poor shadow."

The children maintained their grip.

"Only if you play shadows again and only if you promise to look after your shadow. If you don't, we shall steal it and you will have great difficulty finding it again," said the children.

Sholdan promised to look after his shadow and befriend it and vowed to play shadows with the children again. The laughing children released him.

Sholdan felt sad at the idea of having no shadow although he had never befriended his shadow before.

"My poor shadow," he said aloud, "my poor neglected shadow, I shall never abandon you again."

He sprinted up the mountain and there he saw the Master dancing on top of a big flat rock. He waited until the Master had finished his dance and clapped his hands, while the Master bowed and smiled.

"And how are you?" the Master enquired.

"Never felt better," Sholdan replied gleefully. "I have made a great friend."

"Who can that be?" asked the Master.

"Why, my own dear shadow, who has taught me so much about myself and how to be happy," he replied, laughing out loud. The Master laughed loudly, too.

With that, Sholdan took off down the mountain, jumping for joy and still laughing, with his shadow running along behind him.

The Trap

The Story Of The Trap Shows Us That:

- We may be afraid of recovering from a trauma or illness in case we lose the support that we have come to rely on.

- Becoming too dependent on others can deplete our confidence, increase our fears and foster a sense of helplessness.

- We can refuse to take responsibility for ourselves.

This Story Helps Us To:

Recover from trauma, bad experiences and painful emotions, like anger, fear, resentment, shame and grief

Overcome dependence on others and develop responsibility for ourselves

Surmount obstacles to recovery, reach out to others in need and let the healing power of love help us

The Trap

All the animals in the forest were contented until the day Kieran the Mongoose got his foot caught in a trap. He had been running across the forest floor, chasing a small white butterfly, when the rusty, vicious trap snapped its jaws shut around his hind leg. The trap was heavy and, as he looked at it, he felt sick at the sight of his own blood flowing from its teeth. His pain was unbearable and excruciating and he felt he was going to die then and there on the cool grass.

Kieran the Mongoose let out some blood-curdling screams and howls that ripped into the very heart of the forest. The forest and its animals had never heard such terrifying shrieks before. Shocked, frightened animals scurried for cover in the undergrowth. Insects burrowed into the earth or hid in the dense foliage of trees. A deathly silence descended on the forest; even birds ceased their twittering and love calls. Trees trembled and bowed their heads down towards the earth in the wake of such terrifying screams.

After some time, Kieran's blood-curdling screams ended abruptly and turned to loud, wailing calls for help. "Come, come, help me, its Kieran the Mongoose, your brother! I'm trapped in some big, rusty, vicious mouth, help me, come quickly, all of you come, and help me, I'm in agony, come and help me, help me, help me!" he wailed.

His cries for help brought all of the animals, birds and insects running and flying through the forest to him. They gathered around Kieran the Mongoose and were terrified and distressed by what they saw. They all tried to help, pulling the trap this way and that, squabbling amongst themselves. No matter how hard they pulled and tugged, they could not seem to release the trap. Indeed, it just seemed to get even tighter and each time they pulled at it, Kieran the Mongoose screamed in pain. Even Mrs Bear, with her big gentle paws, could not budge it an inch.

As the animals looked at poor Kieran the Mongoose and his bleeding mangled paw, they became more and more distressed and started to wail and squeal themselves. They were frightened that Kieran the Mongoose would die and the thought of this happening made them scream and howl even more loudly. The sounds of their distress echoed through the forest.

When Human Man approached the forest to collect his quarry from the trap he had set, his heart almost stopped on hearing these strange, blood-curdling cries. He was so shaken and afraid that he turned on his heels and fled, vowing never to return to the forest again. And indeed he never did.

Kieran the Mongoose didn't die, the other animals made sure of that. He was cared for better than any sick animal had ever been. Carried to the nicest spot at the edge of the forest, he could see the sun shining through the leaves and berries dancing in the bushes down in the valley. He had the best view from the forest. They hunted for his choicest food, they made soft, warm nests for him, and they sang songs to keep loneliness at bay. They stayed and watched over him night and day. The other animals truly were the best of friends to Kieran the Mongoose, their brother.

One warm sunny day, Mr Pig from the Magic Forest came to visit the forest of Kieran the Mongoose and his friends. Mr Pig was dismayed and wept when he saw the plight of Kieran the Mongoose. He demanded silence and called on all to listen, as he declared, "My sow wife has claws and teeth that would rip any trap apart – she is fierce and strong and she possesses the strongest of magical healing powers, thanks to her good kind heart. I will bring her here and she will rip the trap apart and free Kieran the Mongoose's leg." Without another word, he flipped his tail and took off, trotting and squealing, to find his sow wife.

When Kieran the Mongoose heard that Mr Pig was going to get his sow wife to remove the vicious trap, he became despondent. He didn't show this despondency to Mr Pig or to the other animals. Instead, he gave them a grateful, sweet smile. Inside his heart he felt afraid – filled with an unknown fear that stole upon him unawares. "Everything could change now," he thought. "The other animals will not take such care of me any more; I shall be expected to take care of myself. I shan't get the choicest food brought to me every day and I shall have to seek out food myself. I shall be alone at times and not have the other animals to keep me happy and sing songs for me and play with me whenever I want them to. No one will feel sorrow for me any more and they won't gather around me to keep me safe and warm and free from loneliness."

While all the animals were excitedly talking about Kieran the Mongoose's imminent release from the trap by Mrs Pig, Kieran the Mongoose dragged himself unnoticed into some thick dark undergrowth and hid. The animals were too busy laughing and making plans for new games to play with Kieran the Mongoose once his leg was healed to notice him slipping away.

Such was Mr Pig's haste that he was back within a short space of time with his sow wife – her of the strong teeth and powerful claws. Upon his arrival, all the animals began dancing in anticipating of the release of Kieran the Mongoose. They called out to him but he did not answer. Instead, he remained hiding in an empty burrow, trembling in case he might be spotted. They waited all day in the hot sun and all night long for Kieran the Mongoose to appear.

"He must be dead!" cried one little rabbit.

"He must be caught somewhere and can't escape," sobbed another.

"Oh, if only we had taken better care of him and hadn't let him out of our sight," wailed Red Squirrel.

"Maybe I gave him the wrong type of food," yelped one old badger.

Kieran the Mongoose listened to their cries and never made a sound. He said to himself, "I shall make them still care for me as they do now, I shall make them feel even sorrier for me. I don't want anything to change ever. I want to hold on to the trap: that way, nothing will change and I shall stay happy. I have been injured badly and even if my leg gets *completely better,* I still shan't be able to look after myself properly. I shan't be able to get the choicest food; only the birds and squirrels can reach the fruit on high branches. I shall never be able to make nests as comfortable as the bears make for me now. Who will sing sweet songs for me and tell me stories and keep the spirit of loneliness at bay if the trap be removed?"

Disheartened by Kieran the Mongoose's disappearance, the pigs trotted home. The exhausted, disappointed animals fell asleep, huddled together for comfort. Kieran the Mongoose crept out of his hole in the dead of night without awakening them. He was so stealthy that he managed to keep the rusty trap from creaking as he dragged it along behind him. He lay down beside the other animals and slept.

When the animals woke up, they were overjoyed and amazed to see Kieran the Mongoose and they shed warm tears of relief and joy.

"Oh, oh," sobbed Kieran the Mongoose, "the trap caught in some old roots and I spent all day and night trying to free myself."

"Oh, we're so sorry, so sorry," said the animals sympathetically and again began to shed tears, thinking of poor Kieran the Mongoose caught in the old root on his own.

Kieran the Mongoose slanted his dark eyes and smiled coyly. "We shall never leave you again by yourself to be trapped in a lonely place," pledged the animals.

Two little swallows, who had watched everything from high up in a Holm Oak tree, rushed off to get Mr and Mrs Pig without a word to anyone. In a breathless rush, the two pigs skidded their way to the forest of Kieran the Mongoose and his friends. Kieran the Mongoose mustered a sour-sweet smile to welcome the pigs. He felt sick and defeated inside; the other animals were hopping for joy.

Without further ado, Mrs Pig wrenched the trap apart, using dagger-sharp teeth and strong trotters. She was so swift in her action that Kieran the Mongoose had only time to let out one yelp. Indeed, his foot was badly mangled but Mrs Pig knew all the healing plants and wrapped them around the injured foot in a tight bandage.

"When the big moon comes again," said Mrs Pig, "your foot will be better and you will be able to run free again." Her mouth stretched wide with pride and contentment. The other animals all rejoiced and were happy that night. All was well in the forest.

The big moon duly came and Kieran the Mongoose's foot got completely better. He remained unhappy, however, and this unhappiness grew day by day. He refused to hunt for himself or eat the food the other animals had collected. He did not laugh or play any more but sloped around, dragging his *fully healed* paw behind him as if the trap were still attached to it. He spent a lot of time alone. He refused to be cheered up and wore an air of cold resentment.

All the animals were puzzled as to why Kieran the Mongoose was so glum and resentful and refused to partake in their fun or talk to them. They watched in dismay as he skulked around, dragging his now healed leg behind him. Some of the animals began to feel guilty and blame themselves taking greater pains to hunt down his choicest food. They all started to feel uncomfortable around him. Many animals, especially the eagles and bears, began to feel angry and resentful towards him for creating unhappiness in the forest. Nevertheless, Kieran the Mongoose looked so unhappy that not one animal voiced the anger and resentment they felt towards him in case they made him worse.

One night, a violent storm took the forest by surprise. No animal had seen the like of this before. The wind whipped among the sleepy trees, causing them to moan and groan. It shook them violently, breaking leaves, twigs and branches and sending them flying through the air. The animals, birds and insects hid in fear. A Little Firebird got hit on the head by a flying branch and landed on the earth right next to where Kieran the Mongoose was taking shelter from the storm.

"I am dying, I am dying!" she cried. "I can't fly, I can't fly! My head is bleeding and wing is twisted – help, help!"

Kieran the Mongoose listened to her cries and his heart filled with sorrow for the Little Firebird.

"Oh, Little Firebird, I am here, I am Kieran the Mongoose. You *will* be able to fly again. I shall help you; I shall find a way."

He held the trembling bird in his paws. As he watched over her, Little Firebird became weaker from shock and pain and her fragile life began to slip away. The wind howled and moaned, restless among the trees; it snapped even the strongest branches and sent them catapulting into the air. Kieran the Mongoose gently held Little Firebird in his mouth and ran headlong into the howling wind. He ran more swiftly than the wind, being blown hither and thither, and was knocked over at times but he kept on running – running forward, falling, running, falling. His little heart was beating like an urgent drum as he went on stumbling, falling and running.

Finally, Kieran the Mongoose came to the forest of Mr and Mrs Pig. Mrs Pig came dashing out to meet him. He was breathless and sobbing. Little Firebird was a shadow of her former self: her injured head rolled helplessly about, her wings hung loose, she was slipping away. Mrs Pig got to work swiftly. She smoothed ointment on Little Firebird's head, untwisted the broken wing and forced some healing drops into her beak. She hummed and sang softly, rocking Little Firebird gently. Mr Pig and Kieran the Mongoose looked on in silence, waiting and hoping.

"I want her to fly again," Kieran the Mongoose sobbed, "I want her to fly again and be free."

Little Firebird opened her eyes and shook herself and moved her injured wing.

"I *will* fly again," she said, "thanks to you, dear Kieran the Mongoose, and to you, Mr and Mrs Pig."

Little Firebird and Kieran the Mongoose waited two more days with the Pigs so that she could grow stronger. Then they heard their own forest calling them home again. They danced, they flew, and they hopped and jumped, dived and played with the now gentler wind. They laughed and sang to each other. Their joy knew no bounds.

Memories of broken wings and trapped paws were carried away by the wind, leaving only faint traces. They were free now. They were flying, they were free forest spirits again, and they were coming home.

The Small Star

The Story Of The Small Star Shows Us That:

- Loss of confidence and self-esteem can make us feel inferior, and make us compare ourselves unfavourably to others.

- It can make us self-critical and blind to our own greatness.

- We may hide away from others and feel lonely and sad and not sufficiently special.

This Story Helps Us To:

Appreciate our uniqueness, beauty and specialness

Build up our confidence and self-esteem

Develop our talents and abilities

Help others if they become lost and lonely

The Small Star

A very, very long time ago, at the dawn of creation, all the Stars took their place in the heavens to add their light and beauty to the world. Some were very big, some less so and some very tiny. Beautiful and full of light, they shone brightly as they moved, twinkled and danced around the heavens. They got to know each other and became close friends, particularly with their nearest neighbours.

One small Star called "Wanita" became very sad and asked a very big Star, "Lalola", that shone close by:

"Why can't I shine my light as far as you can?"

"Because you are not as big as I am," Lalola replied.

"But I want to be as big as you are so that I can shine my light just as far as you can."

"You will never be able to do that," said Lalola, "you will never be able to shine your light *as far* as I can and I shall never able to shine my light *as near* as you can. We both have the right amount of light that is unique to us so that we shine according to our own specialness and uniqueness."

"I don't like that, I shall only be happy if I can be like you," sighed Wanita.

Lalola tried to make her friend see sense but Wanita kept insisting that she wanted to be bigger, that she would not be happy until she could shine her light just as far as Lalola could. Lalola tried to comfort her:

"Oh, you are so beautiful and full of light and there isn't another Star exactly like you and there never will be and I love you so dearly. How can you not be happy?"

Wanita went quiet and closed her eyes, drawing some of her light inside. She didn't talk any more. Night after night, she drew more and more of her light inside until only a feeble little light shone around her. Gradually, she drew that light inside, too.

Her light did not light up the dark place that she withdrew to. The dark place was cold and lonely and airless and devoid of any spark of light. Wanita huddled more and more tightly into herself, so tightly that she did not feel able to even straighten out again.

Years passed, hundreds of years passed, even thousands of years passed, and she did not stir. She felt something and nothing, she wasn't sure, she felt lonely and empty of light but yet knew that that was where she wanted to be. Such strange confusion she had! Her dreams were no longer of shining and twinkling and seeing new things but were full of darkness and emptiness. Now and then, she thought of her bright Star friend, Lalola, and other Star friends. She didn't miss them; they seemed so far away.

She wondered what it would be like not to exist at all. She knew that there was no way that she could not exist at all. She knew that there was always some way that she would exist, no matter how hard she tried to extinguish herself. She had tried her utmost to achieve non-existence but now knew that this was not possible. She began to cry. She couldn't stop herself; she didn't really know why she was crying and leaking so many tears. Her tears leaked through the crack in the heavens that marked the place of her hiding. All the stars saw them without realising what they were. The tears flooded across the sky, leaving silvery trails in their wake.

Lalola watched them and remembered her dear friend from long, long ago. It occurred to Lalola that the leak was coming from the same place where Wanita used to be before her light withdrew. The silvery trails were coming from that exact spot.

"It might be Wanita," she confided to another Star nearby.

"Who is Wanita?" her friend asked.

"She was a beautiful little Star that shone in the heavens long before your time. She wanted to be big – *the same as me* – and because she couldn't, she withdrew her light. I still miss her so."

"Oh, how sad, how very sad," replied her friend.

Lalola missed her little bright friend Wanita as if she had only recently gone away. Memories of their sweet days together stirred up great sadness in her and she began to cry great big pools of tears that ran across the heavens and leaked into the crevice where Wanita was hiding herself. The rivulet of tears stirred Wanita into some different kind of wakefulness and she unclenched herself. A faint light emerged from her centre and shone out towards Lalola. Immediately, Lalola recognised her light and called out her name.

Wanita came out of her hiding place shyly with her light, like a small bright glowing halo around her. She edged herself close to Lalola.

"I now know who I am and what to do," she whispered to the very happy Lalola. "It has taken me such a long time to figure it out but now I shall be able to help other stars who are blinded by too much light. I shall show them where they can go to in the heavens so that they don't collide with each other. Because I am small, I can shoot across the heavens very quickly and never collide with any other star."

With those words, Wanita shot across the heavens and back again. She was able to duck in and out among the stars without either blinding, or banging into, them. The other stars were amazed when they saw what she could do. Smaller stars tried shooting across the sky like Wanita but ended up colliding with each other and getting frightened. Lalola was so happy to see her dear friend Wanita shining happily beside her once more.

"There is another thing we can do together. Both of us know what it is," said Wanita with a twinkle in her eye.

"Tell me, tell me," Lalola urged.

"We both know how to wake up stars that have gone into hiding because they don't know *who* they are and so are afraid that they are not as good as other stars."

"Yes, indeed," agreed Lalola, "we both know how to wake up these beautiful hiding stars and I would love to do that with you."

When the stars are out, shining their brightest light in the heavens, Wanita and Lalola can often be seen streaking tears across the sky to wake up frightened little stars in hiding. Wanita can also be seen shooting across the night heavens, blazing a little trail of light for other stars to find their way home safely. If you look carefully, you will always see her returning to shine beside her dearest friend, Lalola.

Fire Dance

The Story Of Fire Dance Shows Us That:

- Holding on to old resentment and judgment can harden our heart.

- Releasing resentment and grudges and accepting genuine kindness and friendship can help us heal again.

- Reaching out the hand of friendship to another can bring us many unexpected gifts.

This Story Helps Us To:

Accept help if it is offered no matter what guise it comes in

Let go of rigid views, stubbornness, resentment and bitterness

Recover from loss, grief and rejection when a relationship ends

Build confidence and self-love and develop compassion for others

Find friendship and love again

Fire Dance

An old man, called Emmet Reilly, lived alone in a small thatched cottage in a place known as *The Lonely Hill.* The soil was very poor and few people lived there. The climate was harsh and it rained and was stormy most of the time. Emmet Reilly lived there because he had always lived there and that was all there was to it. He never thought of leaving. From childhood, people had only ever called him Emmet Reilly; nobody ever used just his first name.

He sat alone now in his cottage with the wind howling outside and the night bitterly cold. He had no fire to keep himself warm. The turf was too wet to light and he hadn't collected any timber before the winter set in. He was too grief-stricken at the time to bother with wood for the fire. He trembled and shivered now. He had only a few old rags to cover his tired bones. His old bones ached, he had lost the power of one arm and of late he was so stiff that he walked with a limp. He hadn't slept for a long time. He couldn't even remember when he had last slept. His eyes were red and burning. He tried to remember when he had eaten last and wasn't even sure of that. He hated the nights; they filled him with fear and doubt. He was always expecting something terrible to happen to him at night.

His decline had started when his cow, Maisie, had died last year. He had named her after his Granny whom he had loved and who had died when he was a child. He had rescued Maisie before she would be killed and eaten by his neighbour eighteen years ago. He had paid a high price for her – half the winter's turf for that year. He couldn't think about his cow now without crying. She had given him good milk and real friendship all these years. He still felt annoyed and angry with his neighbour, who had neglected to mend the fence. It was because of the broken fence that Maisie had got into the bog and drowned. He had fought hard with the neighbour about that so that Maisie would have some justice, even in death. He couldn't get Maisie out of his head, he felt so bad about it all and he still missed her so much. He had cried every night since she died. The neighbour offered another cow to compensate him in some way but he didn't want that.

He felt so weak that he thought it would be a good idea to eat. He let the idea pass quickly because he had no fire to cook the porridge, which was his only staple food now. He slumped in his chair, with tears falling down his face, wondering how it had all come to this.

A sudden rustling noise caused him to sit bolt upright and look around the candlelit room. Seated on his old stool near where a good fire should have been burning was a small fairy dressed in a long black gown and black hat. The fairy was really beautiful and his eyes were bright and shining.

"Who are you?" asked Emmet Reilly, suspicion rising in him.

"I am a prince," said the fairy. "My clan are out fighting and killing. It's all very unjust and I want no part in it."

The fairy looked Emmet Reilly up and down.

"You are not in good shape yourself," he said.

"Could be better," said Emmet Reilly guardedly.

"Can I take off my cloak and mask?" asked the fairy. "I feel that I can be myself with you."

"As you want," said Emmet Reilly, looking confused and perplexed.

The fairy took off his cloak and mask. Underneath was a small fairy in tatters.

His face was red and bruised and covered in scars. His eyes were red and he began to cry.

"Who did this to you?" Emmet Reilly asked gently and sympathetically.

"Well, lots of people, since I was young, till now. I have been through my own wars."

Emmet Reilly felt very sad for the fairy.

"This is the first time," said the fairy, "that I have been able to take off the mask and cloak."

Before Emmet Reilly could say another word, a dashing young fairy on horseback appeared, dressed in white armour and carrying a red sword. He charged around the kitchen, striking out with his fiery sword at imaginary foes.

"And who are *you*?" said Emmet Reilly to this gallant young figure.

"My name," he answered proudly, "is Justice. I am the defender of the innocent, the broken and the weak. I stand for honour and bravery."

He jumped off his horse and sat down beside the small, frightened, bruised fairy. He reached out and held his hand. Emmet Reilly wanted to do the same but felt too embarrassed to do so.

A third fairy appeared out of nowhere, dressed in a flowing silver gown. He dashed around frantically at top speed. Sometimes, it looked as though he were spinning in the air. He had a mischievous grin on his little face. Again, Emmet Reilly asked for an introduction.

My name is Quicksilver. "I am the invisible force. I am he who mends the broken and sends them on their way. I am a friend to the strong and to the weak. I can rise up high and fall down low. I play in the shadows and hide in the light. I arrive in unexpected places and sometimes come uninvited."

The first fairy got up and put on his little black cape and mask. Justice stood up, too. The three fairies stood close and put their arms around each other. They walked slowly clockwise in a circle. A bright fiery flame appeared in the centre of their circle, and then a very strange thing happened. The three merged into one fairy.

This fairy was dressed in red robes. His face was strong and powerful; he looked majestic. A red glowing crown with stars adorned his head. His smile lit up the impoverished room. He carried a sword that at times appeared brilliant white, at times glowing red and at times sparkling dancing, silver.

He touched Emmet Reilly's dead turf in the fireplace and, within seconds, a warm glowing fire burned brightly. He touched Emmet Reilly gently with his sword and Emmet Reilly felt a surge of energy and renewed strength flow through his body. He stood upright, sure and strong and raised his now powerful arm in salute to the fairy. The fairy waved his sword again and a great feast appeared. Both the fairy and Emmet Reilly ate to their heart's content.

"Why are you so kind to me?" asked Emmet Reilly.

"Well, a long time ago, you saved our fairy mound when 'your kind' wanted to dig it up. We fairies never ever forget a good turn."

Emmet Reilly nodded and they continued to eat of the fine food. The fairy interrupted this contented silence:

"The old lady called Ellie Ginty, who lives down the bog lane, is having trouble with her chimney. Would you be willing to help her?" asked the fairy. Emmet Reilly felt a stirring in his heart and a whisper from his slumbering compassionate spirit. The mischievous fairy winked at him and a big smile spread across his face.

"I shall go down right now and help her," said Emmet Reilly with a twinkle in his eye.

Some days later, the fairies looked through Ellie Ginty's window and there sat Emmet Reilly and Ellie having a feast of porridge, soda bread and jam with a blazing fire in the hearth. The fairy smiled and winked at Emmet Reilly through the window.

A week later the fairy appeared again and told Emmet Reilly that the neighbour he had had the dispute with over Maisie was very lonely and sad. Emmet Reilly's forgiving spirit charged him with urgency and he ran to get his neighbour.

That very night, the fairies looked through Emmet Reilly's window and saw Emmet Reilly, Ellie Ginty and the neighbour feasting in front of a blazing bright fire. They were enjoying themselves to the full. The fairies caught Emmet Reilly's eye and waved at him. He winked back, with a big smile lighting up his face.

Lightning Source UK Ltd.
Milton Keynes UK
UKOW03f2243060314

227704UK00001B/12/P